TANKS ON A SPACESHIP

By

Ryan Michael Upton

Table of Contents

COPYRIGHT PAGE

TANKS ON A SPACESHIP

ISBN 978-1-7645764-1-3 (Paperback)

First published in Australia in 2026.

Kindle Edition.

Cover design and illustrations by the author.

INTRODUCTION

In the outer dark beyond Pluto's orbit, distance is measured in fuel margins, and silence is measured in consequences.

Tanks on a Spaceship is a hard science fiction novella about contracts written in numbers and the people forced to live inside them. When independent operators Jennifer and Ryan are sent to evaluate the derelict vessel *Hammerhead*, they expect mechanical failure, system decay, maybe even sabotage. What they uncover instead is colder: a mission engineered without a return.

At the center of the drifting ship lies a simple equation: thirty-three thousand crew members placed into cryogenic sleep, a propulsion system deliberately underfunded for the journey home, and a corporate directive that values completion over survival. When one officer wakes and shuts the vessel down, the illusion of accident fractures, revealing a design far more calculated than malfunction.

This story explores the fault line between asset and human, efficiency and ethics, obedience and choice. In a frontier where gravity can be manufactured but accountability cannot, survival becomes an act of resistance.

Because in deep space, the most dangerous failure isn't technical.

It's intentional.

CHAPTER ONE

The Dark Beyond the Charts

Somewhere in the deepest, darkest part of the Solar System, far beyond the polite orbits and well-travelled lanes, there was a place no honest navigator willingly plotted.

That was where Jennifer and Ryan were headed.

The stars thinned as the *Space Pirate* cut through the black, its hull humming with the low, steady confidence of a ship that had survived things it shouldn't have. Outside the forward viewport, the void broke into fragments of light and shadow, like a shattered chessboard drifting in slow motion. Radiation ghosts. Ice debris. Old wreckage ground so fine it glittered.

Pluto lay ahead.

Not the quiet dwarf planet from outdated textbooks, but something older, sharper. A threshold.

Jennifer stood with her arms folded, eyes fixed on the approach vector scrolling across the glass. Her jaw was set in that way Ryan knew meant she was already three moves ahead of everyone else in the system.

Ryan leaned back in the pilot's chair, boots hooked under the console rail, grinning like a man about to win or lose everything.

"Well," he said, "last chance to turn around and open a juice bar on Europa."

Jennifer didn't look at him.

"Shields to landing configuration," she said. "And Retract the wing-robots."

Ryan tapped the controls. Panels shifted. Mechanical wings folded inward with a soft clatter of locking joints. Outside, shield drones peeled away from the hull and vanished into the dark, obedient as trained hawks.

"Robots retracted," he said. "Wings folded. Try not to get us arrested in the first five minutes?"

"No promises."

CHAPTER TWO

The Descent

The *Space Pirate* rolled, nose dipping as Pluto's surface filled the viewport with an alien landscape of ice plains, fractured ridges, and scars that looked less geological and more… deliberate.

The cockpit lights dimmed automatically. Instrument panels glowed with mismatched tech: stolen military displays beside hand-wired pirate upgrades. A single jump seat sat empty behind them, waiting for the next mistake that would require a third crew member.

Atmospheric resistance kissed the hull.

The ship shuddered, not fear, just acknowledgement.

Ryan guided them down through a spiraling entry corridor marked only by floating beacons and half-functional satellites. Old security. Old warnings. The kind no one maintained anymore because anyone dumb enough to ignore them didn't live long.

Below, the city emerged.

Pluto wasn't built *on* the ice; it was carved *into* it. Towers rose from circular impact basins, thin and needle-sharp, surrounded by rings of frozen vapor and landing scars. At the center of it all stood a spire so tall it pierced the sky haze like a blade.

Ryan whistled.

“Still ugly,” he said fondly.

Jennifer finally smiled.

CHAPTER THREE

Port of Liars

They touched down in a landing basin already crowded with ships that looked like they'd been assembled from arguments and bad decisions. Cargo haulers with patched hulls. Needlecraft bristling with hidden weapons. Sleek couriers that screamed *trouble* without saying why.

Above them, artificial moons drifted, relay hubs, defense platforms, surveillance eyes pretending not to watch.

Pluto was the gateway to the stars.

And it charged a toll.

As the engines powered down, Jennifer checked her sidearm and adjusted the insignia on her jacket, just enough to be unclear. Ryan flipped his collar up and put on his best "harmless idiot" smile.

From here on out, reputation mattered more than weapons.

Because Pluto was packed full of thieves, con artists, smugglers, mercenaries, information brokers, and the worst of the worst.

The ones smart enough to survive.

Jennifer looked out at the city and said quietly,

"Whatever we're looking for… It's here."

Ryan stood, stretching.

"Then let's go steal it."

Outside, the spire loomed.

Above them, the stars waited.

And Pluto watched, patient, hungry, and very much awake.

CHAPTER FOUR

Touchdown, Rough and Ready

The *Space Pirate* descended like a scar through the dark.

From above, it didn't look elegant. It looked *stubborn.*

Its white hull was scarred and patched, a mosaic of old paint, newer welds, and warning decals that had long since lost their original meaning. Yellow wing panels bore crude smiley faces, half graffiti, half threat, each marked with a small black X like a promise that something had once gone very wrong there.

Twin intakes flared red as the engines throttled down, fighting Pluto's thin, treacherous gravity. The folded wing-robots stayed locked tight against the hull, their joints sealed, their sensors dark and waiting.

Jennifer felt the vibration through her boots before the landing gear even deployed.

"Steady," she said, one hand braced against the console.

Ryan obliged, mostly. The ship yawed slightly, corrected, then dropped the last few meters with a heavy *thump* that echoed across the basin. Ice dust exploded outward in a slow, shimmering cloud, lit by the red glow of engine exhaust.

The *Space Pirate* settled.

For a moment, nothing moved.

Then the engines wound down with a tired whine, like an old animal finally allowed to rest.

Ryan exhaled. "She still knows how to put her feet down."

Jennifer glanced at the hull status readout, scratches, minor heat scoring, nothing new. The ship had landed a thousand times like this, on a thousand worlds that hadn't wanted her there.

Outside, the darkness pulled back just enough to reveal other ships watching. Not openly. Not aggressively. Just enough to memorize silhouettes, registry shapes, and weapon ports.

The smiley faces on the wings stared back.

Somewhere in the city, deals were already being recalculated.

Jennifer keyed the internal lights to standby and headed for the hatch.

"Once we step outside," she said, "we're not just travelers anymore."

Ryan followed, pulling on his jacket.

"No," he agreed. "We're competition."

The hatch hissed open.

Cold air spilled in thin, sharp, metallic. Pluto’s air always smelled like machinery and old lies.

The *Space Pirate* rested behind them, engines cooling, scars visible, unapologetic.

And the city waited.

CHAPTER FIVE

The Welcome Committee

The station rose around them like a rib cage.

Pluto's primary transit hall was massive, too massive to feel safe. Thick walls curved overhead, layered with conduits, vents, and half-forgotten architecture from earlier expansions. Circular ports dotted the structure like unblinking eyes, some lit, some dark, all watching. Overhead walkways crisscrossed at sharp angles, casting long shadows that never quite stayed still.

And beneath it all.

People.

A dense, shifting mass of bodies filled the lower level. Traders, dockhands, couriers, refugees, mercenaries. The crowd moved as one dark shape, slow and restless, murmuring in dozens of languages. No one pushed. No one lingered. Everyone knew better.

Jennifer paused at the edge of the platform and scanned the hall.

"Wow," she said softly. "This place looks packed."

Ryan didn’t answer right away. He was counting uniforms.

Station security stood at regular intervals along the walls and at access points, in dark coats and identical caps, hands clasped behind their backs. Not many. They didn’t need many. Their stillness did the work for them.

“Look closer,” Ryan murmured. “Those aren’t guards.”

Jennifer tilted her head. “They look like guards.”

“They’re reminders.”

Before she could respond, the crowd parted.

Not dramatically. Not obviously. Just enough to create a narrow corridor of space leading straight toward them.

A single figure approached.

He wore a long, dark coat that swallowed the light, its lines too clean for dock duty. His cap sat low, precise. His face was calm, in a way that suggested practice: neutral, professional, unbothered by the weight of the place.

He stopped exactly three steps away.

“Jennifer. Ryan,” he said evenly. “We have been expecting you.”

Jennifer raised an eyebrow behind her dark lenses. “Always nice to feel wanted.”

The man ignored the comment.

“Please follow me,” he continued. “The station commander would like to see you. Immediately.”

Ryan glanced past him at the crowd, at the guards, at the doors that suddenly felt very far away. “And if we don’t?” he asked.

The man’s expression didn’t change.

“Then this becomes… inefficient.”

Jennifer smiled, slow and deliberate.

“Lead the way.”

The officer turned, already certain of their compliance, and began walking. The corridor through the crowd opened again, swallowing them as they followed.

Behind them, the noise of the station resumed, but quieter now, more cautious.

Somewhere above, unseen cameras adjusted their focus.

And whatever deal Jennifer and Ryan thought they were here to make?

Pluto had already made the first move.

CHAPTER SIX

Eyes in the Crowd

Jennifer stopped walking.

Not abruptly. Not enough to draw attention. Just enough to feel the weight of the space around her.

She stood with her hands on her hips, shoulders squared, one foot slightly back, the posture of someone relaxed enough to be dangerous. The cut of her jacket hugged her frame, dark and fitted, its fasteners catching the station light like small, deliberate punctuation marks. She turned her head just enough to look over her shoulder.

The crowd behind them had thickened.

Not closer, *denser*.

Shadows layered over shadows, faces half-seen and half-imagined. Some people pretended not to look. Others didn't bother pretending at all. Fingers tapped at wrists. A few hands stayed buried in coats a little too long. Someone laughed too loudly, somewhere off to the side, and no one joined in.

Ryan leaned in slightly, keeping his voice low.

"With so many people here," he said, "there is bound to be some unsavory types."

Jennifer's mouth curved into something that might have been a smile.

"Only some?" she murmured.

She scanned reflections instead of faces, polished wall panels, viewport glass, and the faint sheen of the floor. That was where you saw intent before action. That was where weapons announced themselves.

Three potential problems.

One definite professional.

One wildcard who hadn't decided yet.

The officer leading them didn't slow down. Didn't turn around. He knew exactly what was happening behind him and exactly how little help he'd offer if things went sideways.

Jennifer straightened and resumed walking.

"If they're watching us," she said quietly, "let them."

Ryan adjusted his jacket, eyes forward. "Confidence," he said. "Or bait."

"Same thing, depending on who's hungry."

They moved as once again, cutting a clean line through the noise and bodies. The crowd shifted to accommodate them, instinctively aware that some kinds of trouble were best observed from a distance.

Above, the station lights flickered once just enough to remind everyone that Pluto noticed everything.

And somewhere in that mass of unsavory types, someone had already decided:

Jennifer and Ryan weren’t just visitors.

They were an opportunity.

CHAPTER SEVEN

Stone and Sound

The corridor opened into something that had once been a cathedral.

Jennifer slowed despite herself.

Towering arches climbed upward, ribbed with age and patchwork repairs, their lines converging far above where the ceiling disappeared into shadow. The real stone, hauled here at impossible cost, was cracked and reinforced with metal braces, cables, and embedded lighting strips that hummed softly like a second heartbeat.

This place had been built for belief.

Now it was used for relief.

After working hard mining the Kuiper Belt, most people came to Pluto to forget. The city had learned early what exhaustion wanted: noise, light, and permission. Somewhere beyond the arches, music thumped through the walls, deep bass vibrations that crawled up through the floor and into the bones. Laughter echoed. So did shouting. So did things become harder to name?

Two figures walked ahead of them, silhouettes framed by the archway, already loosening their posture as they entered the glow beyond. Drinks waited. Debts would follow.

Ryan craned his neck, taking it all in.

"Funny," he said. "You build something like this to reach the stars… and people use it to come down."

Jennifer ran her fingers lightly along a wall as she passed. The stone was cold, but worn smooth in places by countless hands.

"Nothing wrong with needing an off switch," she said. "As long as you remember where you left the on button."

Their escort kept moving, boots clicking softly against the old floor. He didn't acknowledge the music, or the architecture, or the weight of history pressing in from every side. He walked this route like a man immune to awe or trained not to feel it.

The arches narrowed as they went deeper.

The noise faded, replaced by quieter sounds: distant machinery, ventilation sighs, the low murmur of private conversations behind thick doors. This was the spine of the station, where pleasure and power intersected and neither trusted the other.

Jennifer glanced up one last time before the ceiling dropped lower.

Places like this always started as sanctuaries, she thought.

And they always ended as marketplaces.

Ahead, a set of reinforced doors waited unmarked, heavy, and very much not public.

The officer reached for the access panel.

"Here we are," he said.

And whatever version of Pluto they thought they understood.

It was about to get revised.

CHAPTER EIGHT

Familiar Trouble

She stepped out of the noise like it had pushed her forward.

Music throbbed somewhere behind her, distorted by thick walls and too much drink. The air smelled sweeter here: spilled alcohol, artificial fruit, something burnt underneath. Light washed over her in soft pulses, catching on dark fabric and bare skin.

She tilted her head, smiling as if the world were slightly crooked.

"Oh. Wow," she said.

Her voice carried the loose warmth of someone several decisions past sober.

"Hey, you guys," she went on, blinking as if adjusting focus. "Uh… wow."

Jennifer froze.

The woman swayed gently, long dark hair falling over one shoulder, a heavy ring resting at her throat like a claim. Her dress clung and tore in deliberate places, fashion halfway to defiance. One hand hung at her side, fingers loose, holding something small and dark she didn't quite seem to remember was there.

"I am *sooo* drunk," she announced cheerfully.

Ryan's breath caught before he could stop it.

"…You've got to be kidding me."

The woman squinted at him, then smiled wider. "Oh! You *do* remember me," she said, pleased. "That's good. That's really good."

Jennifer studied her face, her eyes dulled by alcohol but not absent, confidence worn like muscle memory. This wasn't a random distraction. This was history walking on unsteady legs.

"Do you know," the woman continued, leaning in a little too close, lowering her voice conspiratorially, "where I can… you know…"

She gestured vaguely, then laughed at herself.

"Never mind. I'll remember."

She straightened, wobbling only slightly, and looked between them.

"What are you doing here?" she asked.

Ryan met Jennifer's eyes for half a second. Long enough to confirm what they were both thinking.

Of all the places in the Solar System. Of all the moments.

Pluto had decided to remind them who they used to be.

Jennifer exhaled slowly and said, “That depends.”

On what you remember.

On who’s watching.

And on how much trouble you’re about to bring with you.

CHAPTER NINE

Cause, Effect, Office Door

It happened quickly. Too quickly for an apology.

The woman lunged, not quite falling, not quite steady, arms flaring as she tried to grab Ryan's sleeve. Her balance betrayed her mid-step.

Jennifer didn't hesitate.

She caught the woman by the shoulder, spun her once, and shoved her backward just hard enough to break momentum without sending her to the floor.

"Get out of here," Jennifer snapped. "You worthless drunk."

The word *worthless* landed harder than the push.

The woman staggered, blinked, and then laughed loudly and sharply, a little broken. Someone in the crowd whooped. Someone else shouted something encouraging. Chaos flirted with escalation.

Ryan stepped in instantly, palms out.

"Wow, Jennifer," he said lightly. "Are you feeling violent today?"

Jennifer didn't look away from the woman. "No," she said flatly. "She was super drunk."

The woman pointed at Jennifer, smiling crookedly. “You always were,” she slurred, then turned and melted back into the crowd, swallowed whole by music, bodies, and poor decisions.

The moment passed,

just like that.

And then the door slid open behind them.

Cold air spilled out clean, filtered, sober.

“Inside,” their escort said.

No judgment. No comment. Pluto had seen worse in the last five minutes.

They stepped through.

The command office felt like a different universe.

Straight lines replaced arches. Panels replaced stone. The hum here was controlled, deliberate machinery tuned to obey. Displays lined the walls, each showing a different slice of the station: traffic, security zones, energy flow, crowds reduced to moving dots.

At the center stood a simple desk.

And behind it, a young woman waited.

She rested one hand against her cheek, elbow on the arm of her chair, watching them with open curiosity and something like amusement.

“Welcome,” she said.

Her voice was calm. Not soft *measured.*

“Welcome to the command office.”

The door sealed shut behind them with a final, airtight click.

Jennifer felt the shift immediately. This wasn’t a trap.

This was an interview.

And judging by the way the commander’s eyes flicked briefly to the security feed rewinding, replaying the shove.

They’d already passed the first test.

Whether they liked it or not.

CHAPTER TEN

Terms of Recovery

"I am Commander Campbell," she said.

She didn't stand. She didn't offer her hand. She didn't bother with rank acknowledgments or formalities. Authority radiated from the stillness instead.

"Thank you for coming at such short notice."

A display lit behind her, flooding the room with hard white text and orbital diagrams.

"Five hundred and eighty-four days ago," Campbell continued, "a colonizer-class starship designated *Hammerhead* departed from inner-system space. Its destination was the C-8493-star system."

The name hung there, distant and abstract. "Twelve days ago," she went on, "all communications were terminated."

Ryan leaned back slightly, folding his arms. "Lost contact isn't exactly rare out past Pluto."

Campbell's eyes flicked to him just long enough to register the interruption.

"This is," she said evenly, "when it becomes rare." The display shifted. Numbers scrolled. Mass estimates. Resource manifests infrastructure projections.

“The *Hammerhead* represents a substantial investment,” she said. “Five point six two trillion, drawn from reserve funds. Materials. Personnel. Time.”

Jennifer felt the number settle in her chest, like an extra layer of gravity.

Campbell clasped her hands together.

“Your task is to recover the *Hammerhead,*” she said, “and determine what happened to it.”

Ryan snorted softly. “That’s a recovery operation.”

“No,” Campbell replied. “It’s a liability mitigation.”

Another image appeared, this one unmistakable.

Jennifer’s ship.

“The Space Pirate,” Campbell said, pronouncing the name without judgment. “Fast. Modified.

Independent. And, inconveniently for my superiors, the only vessel in this sector capable of intercepting the Hammerhead before it leaves reasonable tracking range.” Ryan’s smile didn’t quite reach his eyes. “You’ve been reading our brochure.”

“We read everything,” Campbell said. “Especially when it moves this fast.”

She stood now, finally, and walked around the desk.

"A platoon of security personnel will accompany you," she continued. "Along with our corporate legal representative."

The final name appeared on the screen.

"Derek Barich." Jennifer exhaled through her nose. "A lawyer," she said. "On a rescue mission."

"On a recovery mission," Campbell corrected. "He's there to determine ownership, responsibility, and acceptable losses." Ryan laughed once, sharply. "And if we don't like the terms?"

Campbell stopped in front of them.

"Then you don't go," she said. "And someone else will be slower, louder, and far less forgiving."

She met Jennifer's eyes directly now.

"You have a ship that can do this," Campbell said. "And a reputation for surviving things that should kill you."

A beat.

"I'm not asking," she finished. "I'm contracting."

The room hummed softly around them, systems waiting for a decision that had already been made.

Outside, Pluto kept drinking.

Inside, the Solar System quietly decided where the *Space Pirate* was going next.

CHAPTER ELEVEN

Inventory of People

They met the platoon in the hangar.

Jennifer clocked them before anyone spoke, habit, not paranoia. Eight soldiers. Mixed armor generations. Clean weapons. No insignia beyond contract tags. The government issues a statement pretending not to be.

Commander Campbell stayed behind. This was Someone else's mess now.

A woman stepped forward, helmet clipped to her belt, hair shaved close on one side. "Lieutenant Mara Ionescu," she said. "Platoon lead. We're yours once we leave the dock."

"Once," Ryan echoed. "That's reassuring."

Mara didn't smile. "We're professionals. We follow mission parameters."

Jennifer glanced at the others. "Let's hear the parameters in human form."

Mara nodded and gestured down the line.

"This is Corporal Hayes," she said, indicating a broad-shouldered man with a scar splitting one eyebrow. "Heavy weapons, breach specialist. If something's sealed, he opens it."

Hayes lifted two fingers in a lazy salute. "Preferably from a distance."

"Private Chen," Mara continued. "Comms and signals. If it talks, she listens."

Chen was smaller, younger, eyes already drifting over the *Space Pirate*'s hull like she was memorizing it.
"She's loud," Chen said. "Your ship. But in a good way."

Ryan beamed. "She hears that a lot."

"Sergeant Okoye," Mara said. "Medical and zero-g ops."

Okoye inclined his head once. Calm, steady, the kind of person you wanted conscious when you weren't.

"Private First Class Ruiz," Mara went on. "Recon. Drones. Gets places before the rest of us."

Ruiz grinned. "Or instead of."

"Corporal Vance," Mara said, nodding to a pale man adjusting the fit of his gauntlets. "Cyber intrusion. Doors, locks, systems that don't want us inside."

Vance looked up briefly. "Nothing personal," he said. "Machines just lie better than people." "And last," Mara said, "Specialist Novak. Explosives."

Novak raised a hand enthusiastically. "Only when invited."

Jennifer took a breath and let it out slowly.

Eight bodies. Eight opinions. Eight different ways this could go wrong.

"And the lawyer?" Ryan asked, glancing around theatrically.

As if summoned by the word, Derek Barich appeared at the edge of the hangar, in a dark suit under a field coat, a data pad clutched like a shield.

"I prefer 'corporate risk analyst,'" Barich said. "But yes. I'm the lawyer." Jennifer looked him up and down.
"You staying on the ship?" "I'll be observing," Barich replied. "And documenting."

Ryan snorted. "You ever been shot at?"

Barich adjusted his glasses. "Statistically speaking, no."

Mara clapped her hands once.

"All right. You've met each other. We ship out in six hours. I suggest you use the time to decide if you trust us."

Jennifer turned toward the *Space Pirate*, her hand brushing the hull as she passed.

"Trust isn't required," she said. "Competence is."

She paused, then added, without looking back:

"And if any of you break my ship." Hayes chuckled. "You'll kill us?"

Jennifer smiled thinly.

"No," she said. "I'll make you help fix it."

That earned a few real laughs. Even Mara cracked a grin. The hangar lights dimmed slightly as docking protocols began to spin up.

The crew was assembled.

Now all that remained was to find out which of them wouldn't be coming back.

CHAPTER TWELVE

Arrival Briefing

Barich waited until everyone was seated before he spoke.

Not because he respected order, but because he wanted silence.

"The situation is simple," he said, fingers folded neatly on the table. "The Hammerhead has suffered catastrophic failure. It is no longer capable of independent operation."

Jennifer frowned. "You're saying it's dead." Barich tilted his head slightly. "I'm saying it's dormant."

Ryan noticed the word choice. Dormant implied *temporary*. Recoverable.

Barich continued, "Our objective is to reestablish core systems and retrieve the asset."

"The crew?" Mara asked.

Barich's eyes flicked to her quickly, measuring. "Secondary priority," he said smoothly. "Recovery operations always are."

A few people shifted uncomfortably.

Barich smiled, as if he'd misspoken. "That was a joke."

No one laughed.

CHAPTER THIRTEEN

Private Conversation with Jennifer

Jennifer cornered Barich in the hangar while technicians finished loading the last crates.

"You didn't tell them the trip is one-way," she said.

Barich watched a crane secure cargo with practiced interest. "They didn't ask."

"That ship doesn't have fuel to return without the Hammerhead," she said. "You know that."

"Yes."

The word landed with unsettling weight.

"They deserve to know," Jennifer said.

Barich finally turned to her, expression patient, educational.

"Captain," he said, "people don't volunteer for truth. They volunteer for meaning."

He gestured toward the Space Pirate. "Give them a mission. They'll endure anything."

"And if they die?" Jennifer asked.

Barich's smile never reached his eyes. "Then they fulfilled their function."

Jennifer stared at him, suddenly certain of one thing:

Whatever this mission was, it had never been about survival.

CHAPTER FOURTEEN

Cargo With Opinions

The vehicle sat on the hangar deck like a brick that had learned how to roll.

Rectangular. Armored.

Functional to the point of hostility.

"Designation?" Ryan asked, circling it with open skepticism.

"501," Mara said. "Multipurpose surface transport. Sealed.

Radiation-hardened.

Can survive atmosphere, vacuum, and most bad decisions."

Ryan tapped the hull with his knuckle. It rang dull and solid. "Looks like it was designed by someone who hates curves."

Novak patted it affectionately. "That's how you know it works."

The rear panel hissed as it dropped open, revealing a hollow interior with bench seating, restraint hooks, and cargo clamps welded straight into the floor.

Jennifer frowned.

"That's going inside my ship."

"Yes," Mara said. "Along with us."

Jennifer exhaled, then waved a hand. "Load it. Carefully."

The platoon moved fast and practiced. Hayes and Ruiz guided the vehicle as grav-lifts engaged, the blocky transport rising just enough to slide forward. Chen called distances. Vance watched the deck plating as it might flinch.

The *Space Pirate*'s cargo bay yawned open, lights flickering on as if the ship itself was watching with suspicion.

"She's tight," Ruiz muttered.

The vehicle rolled forward, wheels locking magnetically as it crossed the threshold. The deck hummed as it adjusted mass balance. For a moment, everything vibrated in protest.

Jennifer placed a hand on the bulkhead.

"Easy," she murmured, as the ship could hear her.

The vibration settled.

Clamps snapped into place four, then eight, securing 501 to the deck. Novak gave it a testing shove.

"Not going anywhere," she said. "Wish I could say the same for us."

The soldiers climbed in next, stowing gear with the efficiency of people who assumed they'd need it all. Barich hovered near the ramp, looking faintly ill.

"That vehicle doesn't have windows," he said.

Ryan grinned. "Neither does space."

Barich swallowed and boarded.

Jennifer sealed the cargo bay herself. The door slid shut with a heavy finality, cutting off the hangar's noise.

The *Space Pirate* responded immediately, systems ticking awake, lights shifting from standby amber to active white.

Up front, Ryan dropped into the pilot's seat. "All cargo secured," he said. "Including the expensive kind."

Mara keyed her comm. "Platoon strapped in."

Jennifer took her place at the console.

"Undocking," she said.

The ship disengaged the clamps and drifted free, engines whispering rather than roaring. Outside, the hangar shrank, replaced by black and distant pinpricks of light.

Behind them, in the belly of the ship, the vehicle waited silent, patient, built for ground they hadn't seen yet.

The *Space Pirate* turned its nose toward the dark.

And began to accelerate.

The reveal comes with a ceremony.

The lights in the briefing bay dim, and the image blooms across the forward bulkhead: an enormous, asymmetrical ship, scarred and purposeful, its mass dwarfing anything the *Space Pirate* could ever be.

The **Hammerhead**.

Barich steps forward, smoothing his jacket like the gesture might anchor him.

"Before we proceed," he says, "there is a clarification that must be made."

No one speaks. Even Ryan stays quiet.

Barich taps the console. The image rotates slowly, exposing scale markers that climb into absurdity.

"This mission," Barich continues, "is one way."

Jennifer's jaw tightens. "Explain."

"There is not enough fuel," Barich says evenly, "for your ship to return under its own power. Not from this distance. Not with evasive maneuvers. Not with contingencies."

A murmur ripples through the platoon.

"The only viable method of survival," Barich says, "is recovery of the Hammerhead."

Silence lands hard.

Ryan finally exhales. “So, the plan is… steal a ship the size of a city.”

As Barich explained the Hammerhead’s design, including its hibernation decks, rotating greenhouses, and automated maintenance swarms, his tone never changed.

Reverent.
Precise.
Detached.

“The company invested heavily in redundancy,” he said. “Human error is anticipated.”

Ryan raised a hand. “You’re describing people like failure points.”

Barich nodded. “Because they are.”

Murmurs rippled through the room.

Barich raised a placating hand. “This isn’t judgment. It’s mathematics.”

He brought up a schematic of the hibernation bays.

“Most of the crew will never wake,” he continued. “That was always the plan.”

Someone whispered, “Jesus.”

Barich didn’t react.

"Recover," Barich corrects. "From unknown hands. Under unknown conditions."

He gestures, and the image zooms inward.

"The Hammerhead is a colonizer-class ark vessel. Its purpose is simple: reach distant habitable systems and make them permanent."

The hull peels away in layers, schematic-style.

"Most of the crew, over ninety-eight percent, remain frozen in long-term hibernation," Barich explains. "Only a skeleton crew is awake at any given time. Navigation. Maintenance. Emergency response."

The image highlights the ship's midsection.

Large rings rotate slowly, glowing green.

"These are the greenhouse drums. Self-contained ecosystems. They generate food, oxygen, and potable water. They also recycle waste and stabilize atmospheric composition. Without them, the ship dies."

A few of the soldiers lean forward now.

"The greenhouses support the active crew for centuries if necessary," Barich continues. "They are redundant. Armored. And irreplaceable."

The schematic shifts again.

Around the Hammerhead blooms a cloud hundreds, then thousands, of tiny lights.

"The maintenance swarm," Barich says.

"Autonomous satellite drones. They repair hull breaches, manage micrometeor impacts, and most importantly, monitor gravity anomalies."

Jennifer's eyes narrow. "Collision avoidance."

"Yes. At relativistic speeds, debris is lethal. The swarm detects mass distortions and intervenes before impact. Without it, the Hammerhead would not survive interstellar transit."

The image dives deeper, revealing cavernous holds, sealed bays, machines with names no one in the room recognizes. "Terraforming systems," Barich says. "Atmospheric processors. Seeding arrays. Orbital mirrors. Everything required to convert a marginally habitable planet into a permanent corporate asset."

He lets that last phrase hang.

"The company," Barich says quietly, "has invested five point six two trillion credits in this vessel. It is not merely a ship. It is a future."

Ryan crosses his arms. "And right now, it's missing."

"Yes."

"And we're out of fuel without it."

"Yes."

Jennifer looks at the image at the impossible scale, the rotating life, the silent swarm.

"So," she says, "we find it… or we die."

Barich gives a thin, professional smile.

"Correct."

The lights rise again.

No one speaks for a long moment.

Then Novak mutters, "Well. At least the tank fits."

Somewhere deep in the *Space Pirate*, the engines hum steadily, already carrying them farther from any place that could save them except the one they're chasing.

Ryan doesn't bother dimming the lights this time.

Instead, he reaches down and taps the physical model sitting on the table between them, a scuffed, hand-painted replica of the *Space Pirate*. It looks almost harmless at this scale. Toy-like. Lopsided.

"That," he says, "is what keeps us alive long enough to regret this mission."

He turns the model slightly, angling the twin engine nacelles toward the group.

"Fusion drives," Ryan continues. "Not pretty. Not subtle. But efficient. They burn hot and long, which is exactly what you want when the map ends, and the fuel math gets ugly."

He flicks one nacelle with a finger.

“Independent housing. If one goes, the other keeps us moving. Slowly. Angrily. But moving.”

Jennifer watches him carefully. This is the most relaxed he’s looked since the briefing.

“The *Space Pirate* is two levels,” Ryan says. “Top deck is control, nav, comms, and crew quarters—what little comfort we allow ourselves. Bottom deck is cargo, engineering access, and whatever problem we’re pretending isn’t a problem yet.”

Novak raises an eyebrow. “Like a tank?”

Ryan grins. “Like a bad idea that learned how to fly.”

He lifts the model slightly, showing the underside.

“Here’s the part most people miss,” he says. “We don’t have internal gravity plating. Too expensive. Too delicate. Instead”

He sets the model down and draws an invisible line in the air.

“Tether system.”

Mara nods. “Artificial gravity by rotation.”

“Exactly,” Ryan says. “We deploy a cable kilometers long connecting the ship to a mass. Cargo container. Rock. Sometimes another ship, if we’re desperate and rude.”

Barich shifts uncomfortably.

"We spin around a shared center of mass," Ryan continues. "Centrifugal force does the rest. Floors become floors again. Blood stays where it belongs. You can sleep without strapping yourself to a wall."

Hayes frowns. "And if the cable snaps?"

Ryan doesn't hesitate. "Then we're all astronauts again."

The model's tail section is scarred, panels uneven.

"Fusion engines stay pointed outward during rotation," Ryan adds. "They don't fire unless we reel the tether back in. Maneuvering mode versus cruise mode. You learn to plan."

Jennifer finally speaks. "How stable?"

Ryan meets her eyes. "Stable enough that I'm still alive."

He looks around the room.

"The *Space Pirate* isn't fast like the Hammerhead. It isn't safe like corporate ships. But it's flexible. It can haul cargo, dock with things that don't want to be docked with, and survive places we shouldn't be." He taps the model one last time. "And most importantly, it can reach the Hammerhead."

The room is quiet again.

Outside the hull, the real *Space Pirate* hums softly, fusion cores contained, tether spools waiting for an improvised solution pointed at a trillion-credit problem.

Ryan leans back.

“So that’s the ship,” he says. “Any questions before we bet our lives on it?”

Time doesn’t pass normally once the *Space Pirate* leaves the dock.

It stretches.

Hours smear together under the steady hum of the fusion cores, the sound becoming less like machinery and more like weather, something you stop hearing until it changes. The ship spins slowly now, the gravity tether fully deployed, a dark cargo mass trailing behind them like a silent moon. Inside, the rotation presses gently against boots and bones, just enough to remind everyone which way is down.

The crew settles into routines.

Jennifer claims a bunk on the upper level; one hand always braced against the wall as if the ship might decide to stop believing in gravity without warning. She reviews mission logs she already knows by heart, scrolling past numbers that all point to the same conclusion: *no margin*. Her earlier anger has burned off, leaving something colder and sharper in its place.

Ryan lives in the cockpit. He sleeps in short bursts, boots hooked under a rail, waking every few hours to check vectors and tether tension. He talks to the ship sometimes, not loudly, not with words that expect an answer, more like reminders. *Hold together. Just a little longer.*

Below deck, the platoon occupies the cargo bay in shifts. Novak runs weapons checks on gear that hasn't fired in real gravity for years. Mara floats tools across work surfaces, recalibrating sensors she doesn't fully trust. Hayes counts rations, then counts them again, as if the numbers might change out of shame.

Barich keeps mostly to himself.

He appears in common areas just often enough to be seen working on updating legal manifests and transmitting encrypted status pings back toward corporate space, which will take months to arrive, if they arrive at all. His voice is calm, precise, carefully stripped of anything that sounds like responsibility.

The view outside never changes much.

Stars stretch into pale arcs as the ship spins. Occasionally, a maintenance drone from the Hammerhead's long-range network drifts past, too distant to respond to hails, its automated routines blind to human urgency. The swarm is still out there, somewhere ahead, faithfully guarding a ship that no longer answers.

Meals become markers of time. Gravity days are easier on the body but harder on the mind. Dreams are worse when your inner ear believes in down.

One cycle, Jennifer finds herself in the observation alcove, watching the tether cable vibrate faintly against the stars. Ryan joins her without announcing himself.

“Feels longer than it is,” she says.

“Always does,” he replies.

She glances at him. “You ever run a one-way mission before?”

Ryan watches the cable for a long moment. “No,” he says. “I’ve run plenty where coming back wasn’t guaranteed. This one’s honest about it.”

That earns a short, humorless laugh from her.

An alert chimes softly through the ship's navigation only, not urgent, but different.

Ryan straightens.

“That’ll be the first gravity shadow,” he says. “Hammerhead’s neighborhood.”

Jennifer’s jaw tightens. Somewhere ahead, a trillion-dollar ghost ship drifts in silence, surrounded by machines that don’t know anything is wrong.

Time, which had been stretched thin, suddenly feels very small.

And whatever comes next is no longer waiting.

The Hammerhead drifts out of the dark like a corpse that never finished falling.

At first, it's only fragments, glints of metal tumbling slowly, frost-coated panels spinning end over end. The sensors light up in confused bursts, tagging debris that *should* be attached to something much larger.

Then the main body resolves.

Silence fills the cockpit.

The Hammerhead's massive spine is fractured, its once-smooth hull torn open in places where entire sections have been ripped away. One of the great rotating greenhouse rings is twisted, half-shattered, frozen mid-spin like a broken clock. Atmosphere ghosts leak into space in thin, shimmering veils, instantly crystallizing. Scorch marks crawl along the ship's flank, not from weapons fire but from stress, shear, and violent failure.

Jennifer whispers, "That's… not damage from a collision."

Ryan doesn't answer right away. His hands hover over the controls, unmoving.

"No," he finally says. "That's structural collapse. Something went wrong from the inside, or something pushed it past tolerance."

The Space Pirate drifted at the edge of the Hammerhead's shadow, dwarfed by a ship that had never been meant to stop.

Jennifer watched the colonization vessel rotate slowly against the stars, its greenhouses forming a broken halo around a scarred central spine. Even dead, the Hammerhead looked patient, like it expected the universe to move out of its way eventually. "It's bigger than the scans," someone muttered behind her.

Jennifer didn't answer. Size wasn't the problem. The purpose was.

The Hammerhead was designed to arrive. Not to wait.
Not to fail.

Barich stood at the forward viewport, hands clasped behind his back, posture immaculate despite the low hum of stressed systems. He looked less like a man overseeing a disaster and more like someone inspecting a delayed shipment.

"Bring us closer," he said calmly.

Ryan glanced up from his console. "Closer to *what*, exactly? Half the ship's gone dark."

Barich didn't turn. "The asset remains intact."

Jennifer felt her jaw tighten at the word.

Asset.

She thumbed her mic. “Thrusters forward, minimum burn.”

The Space Pirate obeyed, easing toward the disabled giant. Hull lights revealed damage that the scans had softened. Entire greenhouse segments torn open, metal peeled back like bark stripped from a tree.

Frozen water glittered in the void.

Ryan swallowed. “There were people in there.”

“Yes,” Barich said. “And redundancy.”

Jennifer finally turned to face him. “That’s not the same thing.”

Barich smiled faintly. “It is to the company.”

The automated satellite swarm is still there.

They move with eerie calm, thousands of tiny machines orbiting the wounded giant, welding, cutting, reinforcing, trying to *save* a ship that no longer knows what it is. Some drones drag debris back toward the hull. Others vaporize fragments that drift too far away, as if cleaning up after a disaster that never ends.

Hayes breaks the silence. “We can’t tow that.”

Mara shakes her head. “Even if we could, the mass Ryan, the tether system would tear us apart.”

Barich steps forward, already pale. "The contract assumes functional recovery. This is salvage at best. The fuel projections."

"Don't work," Novak snaps. "Say it."

Barich swallows. "If we return with the Hammerhead in this condition… we don't make it home."

The words hang heavier than gravity ever could.

Jennifer turns on him. "You told us recovery was the only way."

"It still is," Barich says, defensive now. "The *ship* is the asset. Damaged or not."

Ryan finally turns from the viewport. "No," he says flatly. "The *mass* is the asset. Fuel math doesn't care about contracts. If we drag that wreck, we burn everything we have, just slowing it down."

"So what," Hayes says, voice tight, "we walk away?"

The room erupts.

Voices overlap: fear, anger, accusation. Novak argues they should strip what they can and run. Mara insists the swarm might stabilize the Hammerhead enough for partial thrust. Barich talks about liability, penalties, and consequences that mean nothing this far from home.

Jennifer slams her hand against the bulkhead.

"Enough."

They all look at her.

She stares at the shattered Hammerhead, at the frozen greenhouse ring, at the swarm desperately pretending this is fixable.

“If we don’t take the Hammerhead,” she says, “we die out here anyway. Slowly. Quietly. Forgotten.”

She turns to Ryan. “Can you make it move?”

Ryan exhales. Long. Tired.

“…Yes,” he says. “But I don’t know what will break first. The tether. The Pirate. Or us.”

Silence again.

Then Novak nods. “Doesn’t matter. There’s no other choice.”

One by one, they stop arguing, not because they agree, but because the universe has already decided for them.

Barich looks at the ruined colony ship, his voice barely steady. “Then we proceed.”

Outside, the Hammerhead drifts broken, priceless, and deadly.

And the *Space Pirate* begins its slow approach toward a future that now looks just as shattered.

The *Space Pirate* slips through the torn skin of the Hammerhead like a needle entering a wound that never closed.

For a moment, the stars vanish.

Then the greenhouse opens around them.

What should have been green is white.

A vast curve of land arcs overhead, its horizon bending away into darkness. Trees stand frozen mid-growth, branches crystallized, leaves shattered into glassy fragments scattered across the ground. A lake stretches below its surface, cracked into geometric plates of ice, the water beneath locked solid, pale blue and lifeless. Mist hangs motionless in the air, a ghost of atmosphere that no longer circulates. Ryan cuts the engines to a whisper. Sound dies instantly.

No wind.

No machinery.

No life.

Even their breathing feels too loud.

Jennifer presses her forehead to the viewport. “This place fed the whole ship,” she says quietly. “Air, water… everything.”

“And it died in minutes,” Mara replies. “The moment the hull failed.”

They drift lower, following the curve of the frozen valley. Automated towers rise from the ground, terraforming spires meant to seed weather, regulate climate, and shepherd ecosystems into balance.

All of them are dark. Their control lights are off, their antennae rimed with ice.

Novak scans the terrain. "No landing pads. No active beacons."

Ryan banks gently, the *Space Pirate* gliding over fields that will never grow again unless something changes. "The ship didn't *explode*," he says. "It shut down. That means the core systems probably isolated themselves."

Barich looks up sharply. "You're saying it's not dead."

"I'm saying it's asleep," Ryan answers. "Or in shock."

They gathered in the briefing bay beneath flickering lights that hadn't yet decided whether to fail.

Barich waited until everyone was seated. Not for order because silence made people listen.

"The Hammerhead has suffered extensive damage," he began. "Primary propulsion offline. Greenhouse rotation compromised.

Maintenance swarm inactive."

Mara raised a hand. "Survivors?" Barich consulted his data pad. "Statistically insignificant."

A ripple of unease moved through the room.

Jennifer leaned forward. "Answer the question."

Barich met her gaze. "Unknown."

Ryan frowned. "You're saying you don't know or you didn't check?"

Barich folded his hands. "I'm saying our priority is recovery."

"Recovery of what?" Mara asked.

Barich smiled politely. "The ship."

Someone laughed nervously, then stopped when no one joined them.

"The Hammerhead represents a multi-generational investment," Barich continued. "Its loss would be… unacceptable."

"And us?" someone asked quietly.

Barich tilted his head, as if the question hadn't occurred to him. "You are the means by which the asset is retrieved."

Jennifer felt the room cool.

"That was a joke," Barich added lightly.

No one laughed.

They pass over a maintenance hub half-buried in frost, its roof cracked but intact. Cables snake out from it, disappearing beneath the ice toward deeper sections of the ship.

Jennifer straightens. "That's it. That's our chance."

Mara nods slowly. “If we can bring maintenance back online, the swarm will get instructions again. Hull sealing. Pressure recovery. Thermal restoration.”

“And maybe,” Novak adds, “the greenhouses don’t stay tombs.”

Ryan lowers the Space Pirate, the landing struts extending as they search for a stable patch of frozen ground near the hub.

“The ship was designed to heal itself,” Barich says, more to himself than anyone else. “It just needs permission.”

The *Space Pirate* settles onto the ice with a muted thud, vibrations vanishing into the frozen earth.

The crew sits in silence for a beat longer.

Outside, the Hammerhead looms broken, quiet, and waiting.

Jennifer unclips her harness. “If we don’t wake this ship up,” she says, “we die with it.”

Ryan reaches for the hatch controls.

“Then let’s remind it of what it was built to do.”

The hatch opens with a reluctant shudder, metal protesting metal, and a breath of absolute cold seeps into the *Space Pirate’s* airlock.

Lights spill out onto the ice.

The greenhouse was silent.

Not empty, silent.

Jennifer's boots cracked frost with every step. Leaves floated where air currents once existed, frozen mid-fall like green glass. The lake below was a single sheet of opaque white, split by long fractures that disappeared into shadow.

"No microbial activity,"

Ryan said quietly. "Everything flash-froze."

Mara crouched near a fallen tree, snapping a brittle branch with two fingers. "This wasn't slow."

Something echoed far above them, a low, structural groan.

Jennifer looked up. The curve of the cylinder stretched into darkness, metal ribs flexing under stresses the ship had never been meant to endure.

"This place fed the ship," she said.

Ryan nodded. "And the ship didn't protect it."

No one argued.

Ryan is first through, boots crunching against a surface that was once soil. The frozen ground holds hard as stone, etched with the ghost-lines of roots and irrigation channels beneath. Frost clings to everything, turning railings, towers, and distant structures into pale silhouettes.

Behind him, Mara and Jennifer step out, then Novak and Barich. The rest of the crew stays aboard, sealed in, monitoring life support and keeping the *Space Pirate* ready in case this turns into a one-way trip.

“Comms check,” Ryan says.

“Short-range only,” Jennifer replies. “Too much hull mass between us and open space. But we’ll have line-of-sight relays if we stick to the spines.”

They move out, leaving the ship crouched behind them like a watchful animal.

The maintenance hub they saw from the air rises ahead as an angular structure half-sunk into ice, its geometry utilitarian and brutal. Thick conduits run from it like roots, disappearing into the ground in multiple directions. This wasn’t a single control room; it was a nerve cluster.

Mara kneels, brushing frost from a faded marking near the entrance. “Primary systems exchange. Power routing. Structural integrity.”

Barich exhales slowly. “If this place comes back online, the Hammerhead remembers how to breathe.”

They force the outer door. It opens just enough for them to squeeze through, releasing a whisper of frozen air. Inside, the silence deepens. Their lights reveal corridors lined with cable trays and maintenance rails, all coated in ice. Frost flowers bloom across control panels, locking switches in place.

Ryan studies a schematic etched into the wall. “This isn’t just maintenance,” he says. “It’s autonomous repair coordination. The swarm docks, sealants, field welders, everything answers to this node.” “And it’s been dead,” Novak adds, “since the breach.”

They move deeper.

The corridors open into a vast chamber, a cathedral of machinery. Towers of inert processors rise from the floor, connected by thick data trunks. Suspended above them, on massive gantries, are the dormant control cores. Every surface is rimed with ice, but the structure itself is intact.

Jennifer moves to a manual console, cracking ice away from a recessed panel. “Power’s the problem,” she says. “The core is isolated to prevent cascade failure. We’ll have to restart it locally.”

Mara glances back the way they came. “Once we do, it’ll draw energy from every surviving system.”

“Which means,” Ryan says quietly, “whatever’s still damaged will *move* again.”

They exchange looks. No one smiles.

Barich plants himself at a secondary terminal. “I can reroute auxiliary fusion trickle from the *Space Pirate*. Enough to wake the core, not enough to overload it.”

“Do it,” Ryan says.

As Barich works, Jennifer clears ice from a recessed hand wheel, a physical override, old-school and stubborn. She grips it, muscles straining as it resists, then.

Click.

A faint vibration passes through the floor.

Lights flicker once. Twice.

A low hum builds, barely audible at first, then deepens, resonates, and becomes alive.

“Maintenance core is responding,” Novak says, awe creeping into his voice.

The processors begin to glow, dim amber light spreading through the chamber like blood returning to a limb long frozen.

Mara watches as frost begins to sublimate from the nearest conduit. “It’s working.” Somewhere far above them, deep in the Hammerhead’s vast body, systems stir. Dormant drones receive commands. Sealant reservoirs pressurize. Structural sensors begin to report.

The ship is not healed.

But it is no longer silent.

Ryan exhales, a breath he feels like he’s been holding since they entered the shattered greenhouse.

"Alright," he says. "Now let's see if it can save itself before we run out of time."

Time had a strange weight inside the shattered greenhouse, neither moving forward nor standing still. Frost clung to everything like a second skin, glittering faintly in the light of helmet lamps. Each breath inside the suits sounded too loud, too human, against the vast, dead quiet of the ship.

The team advanced in a staggered line, weapons low but ready, boots crunching softly over frozen soil and shattered walkways. Above them, the curved ceiling vanished into shadow, its structural ribs bent and scarred, reminders of whatever violence had torn the Hammerhead open. Somewhere far off, metal ticked as it cooled, an old, tired sound, like the ship itself dreaming of warmer days.

At the far end of the greenhouse, half-buried in ice and twisted supports, stood the door.

It was enormous. Circular. Built for machinery more than people. The surface was scarred by impacts and rimed with frost, the seams filled with ice where the atmosphere had once screamed into the vacuum. Faded hazard markings ringed its edge, barely visible beneath decades of grime and damage.

"This is it," someone muttered over comms. No one asked who.

Ryan stepped forward, sweeping his light across the doorframe. "Maintenance control should be right behind this. If we can't get power flowing from here… there's no coming back from that."

Silence followed, not disagreement, just the shared understanding of the stakes. Two of the crew peeled off to cover the flanks, kneeling behind broken planters and collapsed conduits, rifles trained down the long, dark approaches. The rest clustered near the door, movements slow and deliberate. Fingers brushed frozen control panels, tapping housings, searching for anything that might still respond.

"Manual release is here," a voice said, strained. A gloved hand scraped ice away, revealing a recessed wheel half-jammed by warped metal. "But it's locked into emergency seal mode." Ryan exhaled slowly. "Then we convince it otherwise."

They worked in silence, cutting ice, bracing against frozen ground, applying force inch by inch. The wheel resisted at first, unmoving, as if the ship itself refused to let them go any farther. Muscles burned. Breaths fogged visors. Somewhere, metal groaned in protest.

Then,

Clunk. The sound echoed through the greenhouse, impossibly loud.

"Got movement," someone said, disbelief creeping into their voice.

They pushed again. The wheel turned, stiff but willing now, ancient mechanisms grinding back to life. Warning lights flickered weakly along the door's rim, dim, amber, but alive.

No one spoke.

With a final heave, the locks disengaged. The door shuddered, then slowly began to part, a thin black line opening at its center. Cold air rushed inward, dragging frost and dust along with it.

Beyond the threshold lay darkness, dense, mechanical, untouched, a place where the ship's heart still waited, dormant but not dead.

Ryan raised his light and stepped forward. "Alright," he said quietly. "Let's wake her up."

The door finally yielded with a sound like a continent cracking.

It swung inward on tired hinges, releasing a breath of stale air that smelled of rust, old oil, and long-dead electricity. Helmet lamps flicked on one by one as the team stepped through, boots ringing softly on metal decking.

The control room opened up around them like the hollowed chest of some vast mechanical beast.

Banks of consoles lined the walls, their surfaces crowded with analog dials, pressure gauges, and thick toggle switches frozen in mid-gesture. Most were dark, their glass faces clouded with grime, but here and there, faint phosphor stains hinted at screens that had once glowed green and amber. Overhead, massive conduits and bundled cables crisscrossed the ceiling, some sagging under their own weight, others split open to reveal brittle wiring. Rust crept across everything in slow blooms along valve wheels, down support pillars, around access hatches worn smooth by generations of hands.

In the center of the room sat a long metal table bolted to the floor, scarred by tools and heat marks. Beyond it, through gaps in the railing, the crew could see deeper into the facility: turbine housings like enormous rusted drums, pipework vanishing into shadow, and walkways descending into darkness where the maintenance levels waited.

“Looks like it was built to be run by touch, not screens,” someone muttered. “You’d have needed a dozen people in here at once.”

Ryan nodded, moving slowly, eyes tracking the layout. “And muscle memory. This place wasn’t meant to be automated, not fully.”

That was when they spotted it.

Near the far wall, half-hidden behind a fallen console panel, lay the maintenance robot. It was roughly human-sized but heavier, its chassis broad and utilitarian, built for lifting, welding, crawling through tight spaces. One arm was twisted awkwardly beneath it, actuator pistons locked in place. Its optical unit, once a bright service blue, was dark; the casing cracked.

“Found our helper,” Ryan said quietly.

They gathered around it, kneeling in a loose circle. One of the engineers brushed away dust and corrosion flakes, revealing faded stenciling along the robot’s side: service markings, maintenance cycles long overdue. A severed cable dangled from its back, insulation chewed away as if by time itself.

“Power failure,” someone said. “Or surge. Maybe both.”

Ryan popped open a panel along the robot’s spine. Inside, the components were dense and orderly, despite the modular power cells, control relays, and a compact fusion-fed capacitor designed to sip energy from the ship’s grid. The design was old, but elegant.

“If we can get it moving,” Ryan said, “it can get us the rest of the way. This thing knows the maintenance sections better than any map.”

Tools came out. A portable light was set up, casting harsh white illumination across the robot’s exposed internals. One crew member rerouted a damaged cable, bypassing a corroded junction. Another gently realigned the bent arm, releasing it with a soft hiss as pressure equalized. Ryan worked on the core, reseating connectors and coaxing life back into systems that hadn’t felt current in decades.

For a long moment, nothing happened.

The maintenance robot twitched.

Just once.

Everyone froze.

Ryan held his breath as diagnostics scrolled faster than the display could keep up. One arm spasmed, striking the floor hard enough to chip metal.

“Easy,” Jennifer said, though she didn’t know why.

The robot’s optics flickered. One went dark.

Then the other focused. A status tone sounded low, functional, utterly indifferent.

Ryan laughed once, sharp and disbelieving. “It’s alive.” “No,” Barich said from the doorway. “It’s operational.”

The robot rolled upright and immediately began transmitting.

Dozens of dormant systems answered.

Somewhere deep in the Hammerhead, something *woke up*.

Then the robot shuddered.

A low hum vibrated through its frame as internal systems spun up, tentative and uncertain. A single indicator light flickered, went dark, then flickered again, this time steady.

“Come on,” Ryan murmured.

The robot’s optical unit flared dimly to life, casting a pale blue glow across the control room. Servos whined as it slowly righted itself, movements stiff but deliberate, like something waking from a long, heavy sleep.

Around them, the dead control room seemed to listen.

Somewhere deep in the structure, metal creaked. A distant relay clicked.

They weren’t alone in the dark anymore, and if they were lucky, they had just awakened the one machine that could bring the whole place back online.

The maintenance robot’s head tilted slightly, optics brightening as Ryan finished patching the last connector. A soft chime echoed through the control room, an acknowledgement tone, simple and unmistakable.

“Unit,” Ryan said, voice steady, authoritative, “diagnostic complete. Priority directive: locate and reactivate all other maintenance robots.”

For a heartbeat, nothing happened.

Then the robot straightened fully, internal motors adjusted pitch, compensators humming as it adapted to the uneven gravity. A thin beam of blue light swept the room as it turned, mapping, remembering.

Its voice, flat, synthetic, but calm, crackled through a dust-choked speaker.

“Directive acknowledged. Initiating maintenance network recovery.” It stepped past them, movements growing smoother with each stride, and disappeared down a side corridor marked MAINTENANCE ACCESS LEVELS BELOW. Moments later, the crew heard the clatter of boots on metal replaced by something heavier: the rhythmic thump of industrial feet echoing through the ship’s bones.

Time stretched.

They waited in the control room, checking weapons, recharging lamps, listening to the faint, distant sounds of the ship responding. Somewhere far below, a hatch slammed open. Later, another. Then another. One by one, status lights flickered to life across the control panels, isolated systems waking up like neurons reconnecting after a long coma.

A console near the far wall sputtered and glowed amber.

“Power’s moving,” someone whispered. “Low level, but it’s moving.”

Minutes later, the first robot returned, followed by two more.

These were bulkier units, scarred and mismatched, their paint flaking to bare metal. One dragged a damaged leg but compensated effortlessly. Another carried a bundle of tools, magnetically clamped to its torso. Their optics glowed in muted shades of blue and green, and when they stopped, they stood in silent formation, awaiting orders.

Ryan didn't hesitate.

"New priority," he said. "Greenhouse breach. Seal the hull. Restore pressure integrity. Then proceed to full ship repair, life support, power distribution, and structural reinforcement."

The robots processed for a fraction of a second.

"Priority accepted," they replied in overlapping tones.

And then they were gone, moving with purpose now, splitting off down separate corridors, climbing ladders, vanishing into access shafts too small for humans to follow.

The crew made their way back toward the smashed greenhouse section, following the faint vibration of machinery coming online. When they arrived, the scene had already begun to change.

Robots crawled over the torn edges of the hull like metallic insects, deploying flexible sealant membranes that shimmered as they hardened. Welding arms flared blue-white, stitching fractured supports back together. Sections of transparent greenhouse wall unfolded from storage racks, locking into place with heavy, satisfying clunks.

Slowly, so slowly, it almost hurt to watch the frost begin to retreat.

Ice cracked and fell from broken branches. The frozen lake creaked as thin sheets of water reappeared beneath the surface, dark and alive. Emergency heaters kicked in, raising the temperature degree by degree. Condensation fogged the new panels, then cleared, revealing green beneath white for the first time since the breach.

“Pressure’s holding,” someone said, disbelief creeping into their voice. “Atmosphere stabilizing.”

A low hum spread through the ship, deeper and stronger than before. Lights brightened. Gravity steadied as rotational systems adjusted, tension pulling through the artificial gravity tether once more.

For the first time since they’d entered the dead vessel, the Space Pirate felt alive.

The crew stood there in silence, watching machines rebuild a world that had nearly vanished into a vacuum. No one spoke. There was nothing to say.

They had come aboard a tomb.

And against all odds, they had turned it back into a ship.

The argument started quietly.

It always did.

They gathered in the now-functional control room, the air no longer sharp with cold, the lights steady instead of flickering. Consoles hummed, ancient gauges twitching back toward nominal. The ship still bore its scars, rusted panels, patched seams, but it was breathing again.

“That’s as far as we go,” Mara said, arms folded. “We stabilize systems, mark the ship, and call it in. This thing is too big.”

Ryan shook his head. “We’ve already crossed the line. The moment we sealed the greenhouse and spun power back up, this stopped being a salvage find and started being a responsibility.”

“Responsibility to whom?” Kane snapped. “A ghost crew that’s been asleep for decades? Or to us, right now, trying to keep from being stranded on a flying city we can’t crew?”

The room fell into overlapping voices.

“Life support alone needs a constant watch.”
“We don’t have enough hands for engineering.”
“If something fails, we won’t even know where to start.”
“You can’t just leave it half-alive.”

Ryan raised his voice. “Enough.”

The displays reflected in his visor as he turned slowly, meeting each of them in turn.

"This ship was built for hundreds," he said. "We're what, nine? Ten? Even with the maintenance bots, we can't run navigation, reactors, hydroponics, medical, and security all at once."

"We don't have enough people," Mara said. "This ship was never meant to be run by a skeleton crew."

Barich didn't look up. "Then wake more skeletons."

"They're not trained," Jennifer snapped.

"They're human," Barich replied. "Training can be accelerated." Ryan shook his head. "You can't compress experience."

Barich finally looked at him. "You compress *risk*."

Silence.

Jennifer realized something then, not with certainty, but with dread.

Barich wasn't improvising.

He was following a model.

Then someone said the thing none of them had wanted to say out loud.

"The sleepers."

They all knew where that led.

The hibernation decks had shown green across the board when power came back online. Rows upon rows of cryo-pods, untouched, waiting. Engineers.

Botanists. Pilots. Families, even. People who had gone to sleep expecting to wake up in a functioning future.

Mara's jaw tightened. "They didn't sign up for this."

"They signed up for the ship," Ryan replied. "And the ship needs them."

No one argued after that.

The first pod hissed softly as it depressurized.

The first hibernation pod opened with a wet, hydraulic sound.

The man inside blinked against the light, pupils blown wide.

"Did we arrive?" he asked.

No one answered immediately.

Jennifer stepped forward. "Not yet."

He smiled weakly. "How long?"

Ryan checked the date on the pod readout.

He didn't say it out loud.

The smile faded anyway.

A second pod opened.

A young woman lay inside, dark hair floating slightly as the gel drained away. Her eyes fluttered beneath closed lids. Readouts spiked heart rate climbing, neural activity blooming as decades collapsed into seconds.

She gasped.

Hands shot up instinctively, fingers trembling as she sucked in air that felt too thin, too wrong. She looked around wildly, eyes wide and unfocused.

“Hey, hey,” Ryan said gently, holding up both hands. “You’re safe. Take it slow.”

She stared at him, at the others, at the unfamiliar armor and tools.

“W-where…?” Her voice cracked. “Are we… did we arrive?”

No one answered right away.

More pods began to open nearby, one after another. Men and women blinked into consciousness, some crying, some laughing nervously, some asking the same question in different ways.

“How long was I out?”

“Why are there emergency lights?”

“Where’s Captain Albrecht?”

“Why does it smell like metal?”

They were dressed in soft shipboard uniforms, not armor. Their faces were unlined, untouched by hardship. Innocent in a way that felt almost painful to look at.

Mara swallowed and stepped forward. "Okay. Listen. All of you."

They quieted, instinctively deferring to a voice that sounded like it knew what it was doing.

"You've been in hibernation a long time," she said carefully. "Longer than planned. The ship actually suffered multiple catastrophic failures. We found it drifting. We've stabilized it, but things… aren't how you left them."

A man near the back frowned. "That doesn't make sense. We were fully operational. Redundancies on redundancies."

Ryan nodded. "You were. Something went wrong anyway."

A woman hugged herself. "How long?"

Ryan didn't soften it. "Several decades."

The room shifted as the weight of that settled in.

Someone laughed, sharp and disbelieving. "That's not funny."

"I know," Ryan said. "I wish it were."

Questions came fast after that, panicked, confused, overlapping.

"Our families?"

"The destination?"

"Is the war over?"

"Why are *you* in charge?"

Each answer peeled away another layer of the world they thought they knew.

They learned about the blackout and the slow decay. The ship is becoming a frozen, derelict hulk. They learned that the crew they remembered, the command staff, senior engineers, were gone. Dead or lost to system failures long ago.

Most of all, they learned that the future they had slept toward no longer existed in any recognizable form.

Some cried openly. Others went very still.

Ryan let it happen. Then, when the storm passed, he spoke again.

"You're alive," he said. "The ship is alive. But it won't stay that way without help. You were trained for this vessel. You know its systems better than we ever could."

A young technician, barely more than a kid, looked up at him. "We've never handled emergency recovery. We were the support crew. Apprentices."

"I know," Ryan said. "You're not soldiers. You're not survivors."

He paused, then added gently, "Not yet."

Mara stepped beside him. “We’ll protect you. We’ll teach you what’s changed. But we need you to help us keep this ship running.”

The hibernating crew exchanged uncertain looks. Fear, confusion, and something fragile beginning to form beneath it.

Purpose.

Slowly, one by one, they nodded.

They were naive. Unprepared. Thrown forward into a broken era that had never asked their permission.

But they were awake.

And the ship, vast, wounded, and waiting, finally had people enough to try to carry it into whatever came next.

The first attempt to bring the engines online failed so quietly that no one realized it at first.

Ryan stood at the central console, hands moving with practiced confidence as he keyed in the ignition sequence. Power flowed cleanly from the reactors, numbers climbed, stabilizers engaged, coolant loops opened. The fusion cores responded, deep within the ship, as distant thunder heard through layers of steel.

Then the displays froze.

A warning bloomed across the main panel, amber turning to red.

ENGINE SYNCHRONIZATION FAULT — REAR ARRAY UNRESPONSIVE

"What does that mean?" one of the newly awakened crew asked, voice thin.

Kane leaned over Ryan's shoulder. "It means half the ship isn't answering the phone."

Mara frowned. "We've got power, we've got containment. There's no reason for the rear engines to be dark."

Ryan pulled up a schematic. The Space Pirate's spine stretched across the display, forward sections glowing green, the rear third a dull, stubborn gray.

"There," he said, tapping the screen. "Signal loss between the midship bus and the aft engine cluster. Either the control trunk is severed, or the engines shut themselves down."

"Automatically?" the apprentice technician asked.

"Only if something scared them badly enough," Ryan replied.

The room fell quiet.

If the engines had locked themselves out, it meant they'd detected something worse than simple damage, instability, radiation leakage, or structural stress beyond tolerance.

Mara exhaled slowly. "So, we don't push it from here."

“No,” Ryan agreed. “We'll go see it.”

The journey to the rear of the ship felt like traveling through a sleeping giant.

They moved through long corridors where gravity was weaker, the artificial pull shifting subtly as the tether system rotated. Lights grew sparser. The hum of life support faded, replaced by the deeper, slower vibrations of massive machinery at rest.

Behind them came two maintenance robots, newly repaired, gliding silently on magnetic treads. Their optics glowed pale blue as they scanned bulkheads and cabling, occasionally emitting soft chimes when they logged damage.

The hibernating crew walked carefully, eyes wide.

“I’ve never been back here,” one whispered. “We weren’t cleared past midship during training.”

“No one was,” Kane said. “Rear drive section was considered… hazardous, even when new.”

They passed sealed blast doors warped slightly out of alignment, insulation peeling like old skin. Frost clung to corners where heat hadn’t fully returned. Every few meters, emergency patch plates marked where something had once gone very wrong.

Finally, they reached the aft access ring.

The door resisted, then groaned open.

Beyond it lay the engine cathedral.

The fusion engines loomed like ancient monuments; vast toroidal housings wrapped in conduits thick as trees. Coolant pipes snaked along the walls, their surfaces pitted and rust-streaked. Massive control drums sat dormant, indicator lights dark, as if the engines themselves were holding their breath.

One of the newly awakened engineers stared in awe. “They’re… bigger than the schematics.”

“Everything is,” Mara said quietly.

The maintenance robots fanned out, extending sensor arms. Almost immediately, one chimed sharply and projected a red marker onto the far wall.

Ryan followed it and felt his stomach drop.

A section of the control trunk had been crushed

and not melted. Not corroded.

Crushed inward, as if the ship itself had twisted around it.

“Structural shift,” Kane muttered. “The hull must’ve flexed when the ship lost rotation.”

Ryan nodded. “And the engines shut down to keep from tearing themselves loose.”

One of the apprentices knelt beside the damage, running shaking fingers along the buckled metal. “Can we fix it?”

Ryan hesitated.

"We can bypass it," he said finally. "Reroute control through secondary lines. But that means going deeper into the engine mount itself."

Mara raised an eyebrow. "You're saying we crawl inside the part that decided it was safer to shut down?"

"Yes," Ryan said. "Because if we don't, this ship never moves again."

The hibernating crew exchanged nervous looks. Fear was written plainly on their faces, but so was resolve, fragile and newly forming.

One of them straightened. "Tell us what to do."

Ryan allowed himself a small, tired smile.

"All right," he said. "Welcome to your first real shift."

Behind them, far forward in the ship, the control room lights flickered, waiting for the moment when the engines would finally answer back.

The door to the fusion reactor took all of them to open.

Hydraulics screamed as ancient locks disengaged, metal protesting metal. The door slid aside a meter at a time, exhaling a breath of stale, ionized air that carried the sharp tang of coolant and burned dust. Light spilled in a dim, amber emergency glow, revealing the reactor chamber beyond.

The noise came first.

Not machinery.

Something small. Uneven. A soft clatter, followed by a sharp intake of breath.

"Hold," Mara whispered.

They stepped inside.

The fusion reactor chamber rose around them like the inside of a hollowed mountain. The reactor core itself sat dormant at the center, wrapped in thick rings of shielding and control vanes, frost creeping along its outer skin. Catwalks crisscrossed the space at different heights, ladders descending into shadow. Pipes dripped slowly where seals had cracked, each drop echoing too loudly.

The reactor chamber was warm.

Too warm.

Jennifer heard the sound before she saw them, breathing, uneven and fast.

The children stared from behind a coolant manifold, eyes reflecting emergency light.

They were filthy. Wrapped in insulation scraps. One clutched a tool twice his size.

Mara lowered her weapon immediately.

Ryan's voice cracked. "Who are you?"

The oldest shook his head violently. "They came from the walls."

"What walls?" Jennifer asked.

The boy pointed.

Everywhere

And tucked beneath a collapsed maintenance platform, huddled against the warmth of residual shielding.

Children.

Three of them. Maybe four. It was hard to tell at first, thin figures wrapped in scavenged thermal blankets, faces smudged with grease and soot. One clutched a broken data-slate like a talisman. Another pressed their face into their knees, rocking slightly.

When the lights from the crew's helmets swept over them, the children screamed.

"Hey, hey, it's okay," Ryan said quickly, lowering his hands and switching his lamp to a softer glow. "We're not going to hurt you."

The maintenance robots froze, optics dimming automatically.

The children didn't run. They couldn't. They only shrank back further, eyes huge, breaths coming in short, panicked bursts.

“Please,” one of them whimpered. “Please don’t turn it back on.”

Mara knelt slowly, keeping her distance. “Turn what back on?”

The child shook their head violently. “The sun machine. It gets angry.”

Ryan exchanged a glance with Kane.

“How long have you been here?” Kane asked gently.

“I,” The child hesitated, then looked to the others, as if checking whether it was safe to speak. “A long time. Or a little time. It keeps changing.” “That’s not possible,” one of the apprentices murmured under their breath. Mara shot them a look and turned back to the children. “What happened to the rest of the crew?” The answers came in pieces, overlapping, contradictory.

“They were shouting.”

“People in black masks.”

“They came through the walls.”

“They took the loud ones.”

“They said the ship wasn’t theirs anymore.”

“They broke the green place.”

“They made the lights go out.”

“They said we were too small to matter.”

Ryan felt cold settle behind his ribs.

“Who boarded the ship?” he asked.

The children stared at him, eyes unfocused, as if replaying something burned too deeply to describe.

“They didn’t have faces,” one said finally.

“They wore voices,” said another.

“They laughed when things broke.”

Silence followed, heavy and absolute.

Mara stood slowly. “That explains the reactor lockdown,” she said quietly. “Manual override from inside. Someone forced it offline.”

Kane looked around the vast chamber, suddenly seeing it differently, not as a machine room, but as a hiding place. “These kids survived because the reactor scared everyone else away.”

The child with the data slate looked up at Ryan. “Are they gone?”

Ryan hesitated.

“We don’t know,” he said honestly. “But the ship is waking up again.”

That made them flinch.

Mara softened her voice. “We’ll keep you safe. But we need to understand everything you remember. Even the parts that don’t make sense.”

The children nodded, uncertain, frightened, but listening.

Far above them, deep in the ship's spine, something shifted. A distant clang echoed through the hull, followed by a low, unfamiliar vibration.

The Hammerhead was no longer empty.

And whatever had boarded her once might not be as gone as they hoped.

They backed away from the reactor chamber slowly with the children, the door sealing behind them with a groan that echoed too long through the ship's spine. Whatever the children were, however, they had survived there; they were not answers the crew could afford to chase right now. The engines were still dead. The ship was still wounded. And the sense of being watched clung to them like static.

The decision was made without ceremony.

They would return to the space pirate.

The journey back felt longer than before. Corridors that had seemed merely abandoned now felt complicit, their shadows deeper, their angles wrong. The maintenance robots clattered past on distant decks, dutifully sealing breaches and rewelding hull seams, unaware or uncaring that something else had already been moving through the ship long before they were reactivated.

When they reached the space pirate, its patched hull lights blinking like a lazy heartbeat, relief washed over them in a way no one wanted to admit aloud.

The rest of the crew was waiting.

Faces were tight. Voices low.

"You need to see this," one of them said, pointing through the forward canopy. At first, it looked like nothing more than distortion, heat shimmer, or dust carried on a weak atmospheric current. But as their eyes adjusted, the shape resolved.

A tank.

The tank didn't move.

Steam drifted from its open hatch, curling into the cold air.

An alien stood beside it, back turned, digging into the soil with deliberate, furious motions.

It paused.

Straightened.

Saluted something Jennifer couldn't see.

Then another alien emerged from the mist.

They argued in sharp bursts of sound, gestures stabbing toward the ground, toward the sky, toward the Hammerhead's faint silhouette overhead.

Ryan whispered, "They're not looking at us."

Jennifer swallowed. “They’re looking *past* us.”

Old. Heavy. Squatting low against the landscape like a predator at rest. Its armor was scarred and dull, half-buried by time or deliberate concealment. The hatch stood open, a black mouth yawning toward the sky.

And beside it stood an alien.

Tall, thin-limbed, wearing a uniform that didn’t belong to any known fleet. The fabric was faded but deliberate, marked with angular insignia none of them recognized. The alien was digging into the soil with a tool that looked too precise to be improvised, moving with calm, methodical patience.

The first alien sighting came as a still image.

A figure stood at the edge of a field near the shattered greenhouse, upright, armored, gesturing violently at the ground.

Ryan magnified the feed. “It keeps pointing down.”

“Territorial behavior,” Barich said immediately. “Expected.”

Jennifer studied the alien’s posture. The frantic movement. The urgency.

“It looks like it’s warning us,” she said.

Barich’s jaw tightened, just slightly. “It’s attempting to delay operations.”

"Or communicate," Ryan said. Barich waved the thought aside. "Delays cost money." The alien jabbed the ground again, harder this time. Ryan hesitated. "What if this planet isn't unclaimed?"

Barich's eyes hardened. "Everything is unclaimed until someone enforces ownership."

The image cut to static.

Somewhere deep inside the Hammerhead, something creaked metal, protesting the stress it was never designed to endure.

Jennifer felt the weight of it then.

The ship wasn't just broken.

It was about to make everything worse.

It did not look stranded.

It did not look afraid.

One of the crew whispered, "That thing's been there a while. Long enough that the ground's frozen back over behind it."

Another added, "We scanned the area, no power signatures. No distress calls. Just… that."

The alien paused, straightened, and looked up, not at the ship directly, but close enough that the implication was clear. Its posture was relaxed, almost casual, as if it expected observers. As if being seen changed nothing.

A silence fell over the pirate's bridge.

Boarded a ship. Children in the reactor. A tank in a field that shouldn't exist. An alien digging, as if it knew exactly where to dig and why.

Whatever had happened to their ship hadn't ended.

It had simply spread out, waiting for them to notice.

The argument broke out in whispers first, then sharpened into hushed, urgent voices that bounced off the pirate's cramped bridge.

"That's not scavenging," someone said. "That's a recovery op."

"Or a burial," another countered. "We don't know what they are."

"Doesn't matter what they are," the navigator snapped. "What matters is they're armed, and we're grounded."

Outside, the first alien stopped digging.

A second figure emerged from behind a low rise in the field, shorter and broader, its uniform darker and reinforced at the shoulders. It moved with practiced confidence, a weapon slung but not raised. When it reached the tank, both aliens straightened and performed a precise salute, sharp and unmistakably military.

That silenced the bridge.

The salute ended. The two aliens began to argue.

They pointed at the tank, then at the ground, and finally toward the distant silhouette of the damaged ship. Their gestures grew sharper, more agitated. One stabbed a finger toward the horizon; the other shook its head violently. Even from this distance, the tension was obvious. This wasn't a casual disagreement. This was command conflict.

"Tell me you're seeing that," someone muttered.

"They know about the ship," another replied.

The crew's argument flared again, louder now.

"We leave. Now. Before they notice us."

"We can't leave. Engines aren't stable, remember?"

"Then we hide."

"There's nowhere to hide a ship this size."

"What if they're not hostile?"

"What if they boarded us already?" someone shot back. "What if those kids?"

That stopped the conversation cold.

Outside, the aliens' argument ended abruptly. The broader one made a final curt chopping motion. The taller alien hesitated, then nodded stiffly. Neither looked pleased.

The taller alien turned slowly and stared directly at the pirate ship.

No hesitation. No confusion.

Recognition.

“They see us,” the captain said quietly.

No one argued that.

Silence fell again, heavier this time. The reality settled in with crushing clarity: they couldn’t run, couldn’t hide, and couldn’t pretend this was a coincidence anymore. Whatever force had boarded their ship, whatever had left children hiding in a reactor and machines wandering without orders, it was connected to the figures now standing beside that tank.

“Alright,” the captain said at last, voice steady despite the fear beneath it. “We prepare.”

“For what?” someone asked.

“For the worst,” came the reply.

Orders followed quickly. Defensive bulkheads were sealed where possible. Old, mismatched, barely legal weapons systems were powered up and recalibrated. The maintenance robots were diverted again, this time to reinforce choke points and jury-rig sensor arrays. The newly awakened crew were pulled off secondary duties and paired with veterans, hands shaking as they were issued sidearms, they'd only seen in training simulations.

No one said it out loud, but they all understood.

They weren't preparing to fight a battle.

They were preparing to survive first contact on the wrong side of someone else's war.

As the crew prepared to deploy, Barich lingered near the maintenance robots.

He ran a hand along one unit's casing, almost affectionately.

"These will survive," he murmured.

Ryan overheard. "What about us?"

Barich looked at him, genuinely puzzled.

"You're not part of the inventory," he said.

Then, realizing how it sounded, he added lightly, "That was another joke."

Ryan didn't smile.

The crew fans out silently, moving the way the old training vids taught: low silhouettes, careful steps, weapons kept close to the body. The perimeter forms almost without words. Each person claims a slice of ground: the shallow ditch by the trees, the line of scrub where the grass grows tall and yellow, the shadowed edge of a dried creek bed. The world smells of damp soil and hot metal.

They watch the aliens through optics and with their naked eyes. The tank squats in the field like a wounded beast, its hatch still open. One alien keeps digging, methodical and intent, while the other paces, gesturing sharply, its movements stiff and precise, military, unmistakably so.

A hand signal passes down the line. **Quiet capture. No shots unless everything goes wrong.**

Two crew members belly-crawl forward, mud streaking their sleeves, insects scattering as they move. Another pair shifts to cut off retreat toward the tank. The rest hold fast, fingers tight on triggers, breaths slow and measured.

The digging alien suddenly stops. Its head tilts. For a heartbeat, no one moves.

Then the second alien turns too late.

The crew rushes as one, bursting from cover in a blur of motion. A stun charge snaps through the air with a flat crack, slamming into the pacing alien and dropping it hard. The digger spins, startled, reaching for something at its belt, but a crew member tackles it low, driving both of them into the dirt.

There's shouting, short, sharp, terrified sounds from the alien, guttural and panicked. The crew pins its limbs, binds them with field restraints, and drags it back toward the trees. The tank looms nearby, silent, unreadable, its open hatch a dark mouth they do not yet dare approach.

The stunned alien lies motionless in the grass. No one relaxes.

They pull the captive into cover, weapons still trained outward. The alien trembles, its uniform torn and smeared with soil, eyes wide and unfocused. It speaks rapidly, words tumbling over each other, pointing back toward the tank… and then upward, toward the sky.

The crew exchange looks.

Whatever boarded their ship, whatever drove children into a fusion reactor and soldiers into a field with a tank, it isn't finished yet. And now, at last, they have someone who might tell them why.

They drag the captive alien into the shadow of a fallen greenhouse strut, the vast interior of the rotating cylinder stretching above them like a sideways sky. Clouds drift lazily overhead, fields and rivers curving up the walls until perspective gives up trying to make sense of it. At the far end of the habitat, a massive wall seals the cylinders, smooth, armored, and far too solid to be decorative.

The alien does not appreciate any of this.

It thrashes against the restraints, face flushing odd shades of green and purple as it begins to shout.

The noises are… impressive.

It bellows in a rapid, sputtering stream of syllables, stomping its foot for emphasis despite being half-pinned to the ground. Spit flies. Its helmetless head, its frill flapping wildly, gestures with its chin, elbows, and, somehow, its knees.

"GRRAAAK—NO NO NO—BLIT-TOKK! BLIT-TOKK!"
It glares at the crew, then at the tank, then at the sky, then at the dirt it was digging. It kicks the dirt angrily, immediately yelps, and hops on one foot while continuing to yell without pausing for breath.

One crew member leans closer. "Is… is it insulting us or the planet?"

The alien hears this and explodes again, pointing directly at the crew leader and screaming something that sounds suspiciously like a very personal accusation involving ancestry, tools, and what might be fermented algae.

When the first reports of alien activity came in, Barich was not alarmed.

He was pleased.

"Confirm hostile intent," he said calmly.

"They haven't fired," Mara said. "They're just… watching."

Barich tapped the screen. "Intent precedes action."

Ryan frowned. "They're standing near the ground. They keep pointing at it."

Barich waved it away. "Territorial behavior. Expected."

Jennifer studied the image more closely, the alien's frantic gestures, the agitation.

"They're trying to tell us something," she said.

Barich's jaw tightened just slightly.

"They're trying to delay us," he corrected. "And delays cost money."

Then the ground vibrates.

At first, it's subtle, just a low, distant groan, like a ship settling under stress. The crew stiffens, weapons coming up. The alien freezes mid-rant, eyes widening.

The sound deepens slowly, rhythmic **creak… creak… creak**, rolling through the habitat. Birds lift from the fields in panicked clouds. Dust shakes loose from the curved wall at the far end of the cylinder.

The alien lets out a strangled noise of pure outrage and terror, pointing frantically at the wall and shouting even louder than before.

"NO NO NO NO—THIS IS *NOT* THE TIME—BLIT-TOKK WALL! BLIT-TOKK WALL!"

The wall splits.

Seams appear where there were none, long vertical lines glowing faintly. With a thunderous mechanical roar, massive sections peel back like armored petals.

And tanks begin to pour out.

Not one. Not two. Dozens.

They roll out in tight formation, treads chewing up grass and soil, turrets swiveling with cold precision. Sleek, angular hulls gleam under the filtered sunlight of the greenhouse, each marked with the same symbols as the alien's uniform.

The swarm accelerates.

Straight toward the space pirate.

The crew stares in stunned silence.

The alien, still bound, throws its head back and screams half fury, half panic, then glares at the crew with blazing eyes, as if this is somehow *their* fault.

"SEE?!" it shrieks, voice cracking. "THIS IS WHY I WAS DIGGING!"

The first tank fires up its main gun.

The greenhouse echoes with the sound of war.

The argument shattered all at once.

Someone shouted, no one ever agreed later who, and the word *tanks* became a scream.

The alien prisoner chose that exact moment to completely lose what passed for its mind. It thrashed against its restraints, four elbows flailing, faceplates flushing from purple to an alarming orange. It bellowed in a language that sounded like a blender full of gravel and outrage, stamping one foot repeatedly as if filing a formal complaint with the universe.

Then the wall *moved.*

The great curved bulkhead at the end of the rotating greenhouse groaned, a deep, stomach-turning sound that vibrated through soil, roots, and steel alike. Hairline seams lit up in amber lines. The creaking became a roar.

Panels folded outward.

And tanks poured through.

Not rolled *deployed.* They dropped from hidden alcoves like insects from a broken hive, landing hard, suspension systems absorbing the artificial gravity as if they had been waiting centuries for this exact cue. Turrets snapped up. Sensors flared blue and red. Tracks bit into the greenhouse soil, shredding grass and irrigation lines as they accelerated straight toward the Space Pirate.

"CONTACT! MULTIPLE CONTACTS!" someone yelled.

Panic became motion.

The perimeter squad reacted on instinct. Troopers splashed through irrigation channels, boots sinking into mud as they spread out, dropping to their knees behind overturned planters and equipment crates. Rifles came up. Power cells whined. A heavy weapon clattered as it was dragged into position. The alien prisoner screamed louder, somehow accusatory now, pointing wildly at the tanks and then at the crew, as if yelling *I TOLD YOU SO* was the most important part of the invasion.

The first shot cracked the air. A lance of energy tore through the misty greenhouse light and slammed into the lead tank's side. The impact flared, but the armor held. The tank responded instantly. Its turret pivoted with frightening smoothness.

The return fire hit a tree.

The tree ceased to be a tree.

Splinters, steam, and leaves exploded outward as the shot carved a smoking trench through the soil behind it. The shockwave knocked two crew members flat. One of them scrambled up, swearing loudly and creatively.

"Fall back! Keep them off the ship!" Ryan shouted.

The Space Pirate loomed in the distance, battered but defiant, its hull catching flashes of weapons fire. Defensive turrets tried to come online. Half of them stuttered, one spun uselessly, and another fired a single angry burst before going dark.

More tanks emerged.

Some unfolded legs instead of tracks, climbing over irrigation berms. Others deployed infantry drones that skittered forward, weapons already hot. The greenhouse filled with noise; shouting, weapons fire, alarms, the alien's nonstop furious ranting.

The alien managed to roll onto its side and continued yelling at maximum volume, now clearly furious with *everyone*, including the tanks, the crew, the wall, and possibly gravity itself. A trooper leaned over it mid-reload and shouted, "NOW WOULD BE A GREAT TIME FOR TRANSLATION!"

The alien paused just long enough to point at the oncoming armor and scream something that, by tone alone, clearly meant *THIS IS WHY YOU DON'T DIG THERE.*

Another tank round slammed into the ground short of the perimeter, spraying dirt and water into the air. The artificial gravity tugged it all back down in a slow, horrible rain.

The crew held the line as best they could, firing, repositioning, and dragging the wounded back toward cover. The Space Pirate loomed behind them like a promise and a liability all at once.

Whatever had been sleeping inside that wall had finally woken up.

And it was very, very angry.

The Space Pirate *woke up angry*.

Jennifer vaulted into the pilot cradle as alarms howled around her, the deck vibrating under distant impacts. A tank round chewed a crater into the soil where the boarding ladder had been seconds earlier. The cockpit sealed with a hiss, the world snapping into sharp clarity through her multi-layered optics.

Her visor unfolded like a living thing, mirrored lenses stacking, rotating, locking. The greenhouse, the tanks, the fleeing crew, all of it overlaid with targeting brackets and threat glyphs. Her breath steadied. Panic drained away, replaced by something colder and sharper.

"Come on, you beautiful disaster," she muttered, fingers flying.

The Space Pirate's fusion engines coughed once.

Then *roared*.

Artificial gravity fought her as the ship lifted, its battered hull shuddering as it clawed free of the ground. Loose soil and shattered greenery spiraled outward as the tether systems disengaged. The Pirate yawed hard, stabilizers snapping into place just as a tank fired again, its shot slicing harmlessly beneath the rising hull.

Jennifer grinned.

"Targets acquired," she said, more to herself than anyone else.

The first turret came online with a sound like a predator clearing its throat.

She fired.

A lance of coherent energy stabbed downward, punching clean through the lead tank's turret. The vehicle didn't explode; it simply *stopped*, armor glowing white-hot before slumping into the dirt like a tired animal.

The rest of the swarm reacted instantly.

Too late.

Jennifer rolled the Space Pirate on its axis, skimming just above the greenhouse canopy. Secondary cannons barked, stitching fire across the field. Tanks tried to scatter, tracks tearing up soil, but the Pirate was faster, an old raider built to hunt things that ran.

One tank attempted to deploy a shield.

Jennifer toggled a different switch.

Missile bay doors irised open.

The missiles were small, inelegant, and extremely rude. They dropped, kicked to the side, and detonated beneath the tank formation, flipping two armored vehicles end over end. One landed upside down, its turret spinning uselessly, firing into the sky in what looked suspiciously like panic.

On the ground, the crew stared.

Someone cheered.

Someone else just whispered, “She fixed the guns?”

Jennifer dipped the nose and brought the main cannon to bear on the wall, the place the tanks had come from. A warning tone chimed, half the system complaining, the other half daring her to try.

She did anyway.

The shot hit the wall dead center. Not a breach, something *worse*. The structure buckled inward, internal supports collapsing in a chain reaction. Whatever mechanism had been hiding those tanks screamed in protest as it tore itself apart.

Silence followed. Smoke drifted. Burning wreckage dotted the field.

Jennifer pulled the Space Pirate into a hover, engines snarling softly, her reflection staring back at her from the mirrored visor, eyes wide, feral, alive.

“Ground team,” she said over the comms, voice calm now. “You’re clear. For the moment.” Behind her, systems flickered, damaged, temperamental, held together by stubbornness and luck. Ahead of her, the greenhouse wall sagged ominously.

And somewhere deep inside the ship, something heavy shifted, as if the Hammerhead itself was deciding whether this fight was truly over.

The Space Pirate settled back onto the torn earth in a cloud of dust and drifting leaves, its engines winding down with a tired, metallic sigh. Scorched tank hulks smoldered in the distance, their heat warping the air inside the vast greenhouse cylinder. For the first time since the fighting started, there was no gunfire, only the creak of stressed structures and the soft hiss of cooling metal.

The boarding ramp dropped.

Jennifer climbed out, visor retracting in smooth segments until her face was visible again, smudged with sweat, hair half loose, eyes still bright with adrenaline. She didn't get more than three steps before Ryan reached her.

He grabbed her in a fierce, almost clumsy hug.

"You absolute maniac," he said, laughing and half-choking at the same time. "You flew it like it *wanted* to be flown."

She laughed back, breathless. "You should've seen the targeting lag. I was basically arguing with the ship."

Ryan pulled back, grinning widely, eyes flicking past her to the battered but very much intact Space Pirate. "Yeah. It argued back… and won."

The rest of the crew began to gather, armed, muddy, bruised, but standing. Someone clapped Jennifer on the shoulder. Someone else raised a fist. A few of the hibernation crew stared at her as she'd just stepped out of a legend; they weren't sure if it was real yet.

The captured alien, still bound and still furious, chose that moment to start yelling again, much less confidently this time. It gestured wildly at the smoking battlefield, then at Jennifer, then made a sound that might have been a curse or a formal complaint to the universe.

"Shut it," someone said, gently poking it with a rifle barrel.

Laughter rippled through the group, real laughter this time, shaky but warm. The kind that only comes after you realize you're still alive.

Ryan looked around, taking it all in: the surviving crew, the fallen enemies, the impossible curve of the greenhouse above them. "We held," he said quietly. "Against *that*."

Jennifer leaned against the Space Pirate's hull, patting it once like an old animal. "She's rough," she said. "But she still bites."

Someone produced a ration flask. Another passed around crushed emergency bars. It wasn't much, but it was enough. They ate, they laughed, they talked over each other, retelling the fight in exaggerated bursts, who tripped, who fired first, which tank flipped the funniest.

For a few precious minutes, the ship was safe. The crew was together.

Victory, small, battered, and temporary, was theirs.

And above them, the greenhouse sky slowly turned, carrying the sun along its impossible arc, as if the universe itself had decided to give them a moment to breathe before whatever came next.

The celebration didn't last long. Victory never did on a broken ship in the middle of nowhere. Ryan cleared his throat, clapped his hands once, and the mood shifted from relief to purpose.

"Alright," he said, nodding toward the bound alien. "Let's find out *why* our greenhouse turned into a tank vending machine."

They dragged the alien over to a half-crushed maintenance crate and set it down. Someone tried to look intimidating. Someone else failed and tripped on a hose. Jennifer folded her arms and just stared.

The alien stared back.

It was… difficult to take seriously.

Shorter than expected, all elbows and knees, it's uniform, rumpled, and clearly not designed for sitting. Its skin shimmered faintly, like oil on water, and its eyes blinked independently, which did *not* help its case. A small crest on its head pulsed red every time it inhaled, which was often and angrily.

Ryan crouched in front of it. “Okay. Let’s start simple. Who are you, and where did you come from?”

The alien sucked in a breath and exploded.

“BLRRRAAAK-THE-SECOND-OF-TRENCH-SEVEN DEMANDS DIPLOMATIC RESPECT AND ALSO A CHAIR WITH BACK SUPPORT.”

“Hard no,” Jennifer said.

The alien continued anyway, flailing its bound hands. **“YOU DESCENDED FROM THE SKY LIKE METAL LOCUSTS, YOU DRILLED, YOU HUMMED MENACINGLY, AND THEN YOUR GIANT FLOATING FARM BROKE MY COUSIN’S WEATHER ARRAY.”**

Ryan blinked. “Your cousin?”

“YES. VERY SENSITIVE COUSIN. HE WAS PROMOTED POSTHUMOUSLY.”

Jennifer pinched the bridge of her nose. “Focus. Planet. Origin.” The alien huffed, crest flashing faster.

“THIS PLANET. THE ONE YOU WERE

ABOUT TO ‘COLONISE.’

WE CALL IT GRR’THAK. YOU CALL IT” it squinted.

“CANDIDATE WORLD EIGHTY-SEVEN B.’ TERRIBLE NAME. NO POETRY.”

The crew exchanged looks. “So,” Ryan said slowly, “you attacked the Hammerhead because you thought we were invading.”

“YES. OBVIOUSLY.” The alien leaned forward as far as the restraints allowed.

“GIANT SHIP. GIANT DRILLS. GIANT FARM DOME. CLASSIC INVASION POSTURE.”

Jennifer gestured broadly around them. “We *crashed.*”

The alien froze. One eye blinked. Then the other.

“…YOU WERE?”

“Yes,” several crew members said at once.

The alien’s crest dimmed to an embarrassed pink. **“OH.”**

There was a long pause. **“THAT… EXPLAINS THE SCREAMING CHILDREN IN THE REACTOR.”**

Ryan stared. “You put *children* in the fusion reactor?”

“THEY WERE VERY GOOD AT HIDING. WE LOST THEM TWICE.”

Jennifer groaned. “I am going to need therapy *and* a drink.”

The alien sagged against the crate. “**LOOK. WE THOUGHT YOU WERE HERE TO TAKE THE PLANET.**

WE MOBILIZED THE TANK WALL. IT WAS A WHOLE THING. VERY EXPENSIVE.”

“You have a *tank wall*?” someone asked faintly.

“**HAD.**” The alien gestured toward the smoking wreckage outside. “**NOW IT IS A HISTORICAL MISTAKE.**”

Silence stretched, then someone snorted. Then another laughed. Soon, half the crew was chuckling, the tension finally cracking.

Ryan stood. “So… misunderstanding. Big one.”

The alien nodded solemnly.

“**ENORMOUS. PROBABLY GOING IN THE TEXTBOOKS.**”

Jennifer stepped closer, meeting its many-eyed gaze. “We didn’t come to invade. We came to survive.”

The alien considered this, crest pulsing slowly. “**…IN THAT CASE.**” It straightened a little.

“**MAY I FORMALLY APOLOGIZE FOR THE TANKS?**”

Ryan sighed. “We’ll… put it on the agenda.”

Somewhere deep in the ship, machinery hummed back to life.

And for the first time since the crash, the possibility of *peace,* awkward, ridiculous peace, didn't seem impossible.

CHAPTER FIFTEEN

Scars That Hold

The Hammerhead did not return to life all at once.
It came back in pieces.

Power conduits hummed instead of screamed. Gravity stopped stuttering and settled into something trustworthy. The greenhouse rotation smoothed, the great cylinder sighing like a tired animal that had decided, finally, not to die today.

The maintenance robots clanked through corridors that still smelled faintly of burned insulation and fear, sealing fractures, knitting metal, repainting warnings no one would read. Every successful diagnostic felt less like a victory and more like an apology from the ship itself.

The hibernation crew is now working beside the veterans.

No one called them "naïve" anymore.

They moved carefully but without hesitation, hands steady where they had once shaken. One rerouted coolant without being asked. Another calibrated sensor, calmly explaining why the readings were lying. A former botanist argued with an engineer and won. They had learned the fastest way possible: by surviving.

Jennifer watched them from the command deck, helmet tucked under her arm, grease still streaked across her jaw. Ryan leaned against a console beside her; eyes were hollowed with exhaustion and something like pride.

“We didn’t wake the wrong people,” he said quietly.

“No,” Jennifer replied. “We just woke them early.”

Below them, the captured alien sat on a crate, bound but far from silent.

CHAPTER SIXTEEN

The Angriest Explanation in the Universe

The alien gestured furiously at the floor.

It stamped one clawed foot, jabbed downward, then made a sweeping motion that clearly meant *all of this*, followed by a sharp chopping gesture that clearly meant *not yours*.

It yelled.

The translation software tried its best.

“UNACCEPTABLE SOIL TRANSACTION YOU ARE DIGGING WRONG. THIS GROUND HAS PERMITS”

Jennifer crouched to its eye level. “You attacked our ship.”

The alien’s frill flared. It slapped the ground again, harder.

“YOU ATTACKED FIRST BY EXISTING ON IT.”

Ryan pinched the bridge of his nose. “That’s not how, never mind.” The alien continued, voice rising, gestures growing more theatrical. It mimed ships landing, drills descending, flags being planted. It shook with outrage.

"YOU CALL IT COLONIZATION. WE CALL IT **STEALING WITH PAPERWORK**."

Silence settled in the bay.

One of the former hibernation crew, young, sharp-eyed, no longer trembling, spoke up. "They thought the Hammerhead was the first wave."

The alien pointed at them enthusiastically. "YES. YOU. SMART ONE." Jennifer exhaled slowly. "We didn't come to invade."

The alien squinted. Then jabbed the floor again.

"YOU ALWAYS SAY THAT."

CHAPTER SEVENTEEN

What the Ground Remembers

The Hammerhead orbited over a pale sky streaked with unfamiliar clouds. The Space Pirate's landing thrusters scorched long shadows across fields that had once hidden tanks behind false walls.

No tanks moved now.

The ship settled with a deep, resonant thud, not a crash, not a victory. Just arrived.

Ramps lowered. Air met air.

Jennifer stepped onto the soil first, boots sinking slightly into ground that had been fought over by mistake. Ryan followed. Then the rest of the crew, old hands and newly hardened ones, together, spreading out with quiet discipline.

The alien stood at the edge of the ramp, arms crossed, glaring at the dirt as if daring it to betray him again.

"Still angry?" Jennifer asked. "YES," the alien said promptly.
"BUT… LESS SHOOTY."

That felt like progress.

Behind them, the Hammerhead loomed scarred, repaired, alive. A ship that had survived panic, misunderstanding, and war is now choosing to rest.

The hibernation crew moved confidently through the unloading process, calling out measurements, adapting plans, and correcting each other without fear. Whatever innocence they had lost, they had replaced it with something stronger.

Capability.

Jennifer looked back at the ship, then at the planet.

“Let’s do this properly,” she said.

The alien nodded once, stiffly. “GOOD,” it replied. “AND STOP DIGGING THERE. THAT IS A HISTORIC ROCK.”

The crew paused.

Jennifer smiled.

CHAPTER EIGHTEEN

The Shape of the Lie

Barich had been quiet for too long.

Jennifer noticed it first, not because he said nothing, but because he stopped *pretending* to listen. He stood apart from the others in the Hammerhead's control room, data pad glowing faintly against his chest, eyes tracking numbers no one else could see.

The ship hummed steadily now. The atmospheric circulation had resumed. Temperature gradients stabilized. The maintenance robots moved with purpose instead of desperation.

They had done it.

And Barich looked… satisfied.

Not relieved.

Not grateful.

Satisfied.

Ryan leaned close to Jennifer. "You feel that?"

She nodded. "He got what he wanted."

Barich cleared his throat.

"Now that the Hammerhead is operational," he said smoothly, "we need to discuss command authority."

The room went still.

Mara folded her arms. "Command authority already exists."

"Yes," Barich agreed, smiling thinly. "Corporate authority."

He tapped his data pad. Several consoles flickered, then locked.

Jennifer swore as her station went dark.

"What did you do?" Ryan demanded.

"I enacted the final clause of my contract," Barich replied calmly. "Asset reclamation."

Red text crawled across the main display:

CORPORATE OVERRIDE — ACTIVE

"Barich," Jennifer said slowly, "undo that."

"I'm afraid I can't," he replied. "You see, the mission was never recovery *with the crew*. It was a recovery *of property*."

CHAPTER NINETEEN

Disposable Variables

Weapons came up.

Barich didn't flinch.

"You can shoot me," he said. "But it won't change anything. The Hammerhead now recognizes *me* as primary operator."

Ryan stared at the screen. "You told us this was one way."

Barich nodded. "That part was true."

Mara's voice was ice. "You sent us here knowing we wouldn't be coming back."

"I sent you here knowing *someone* wouldn't," Barich corrected. "Your ship, however, was always irrelevant."

The realization hit hard.

The Space Pirate.

The fuel math.

The insistence that only the Hammerhead could save them.

Jennifer's fists clenched. "You used us as a tug."

"Yes," Barich said. "A very clever one."

He turned toward the viewport, where the planet curved below them, green, alive, *claimed.*

"The company discovered this world decades ago," Barich continued. "Long before the Hammerhead launched.

Unfortunately, it was… already occupied."

Ryan's voice was tight. "The aliens."

"They objected to our presence," Barich said. "Negotiations failed. So the Hammerhead was sent under the guise of colonization while our competitors were distracted elsewhere."

Mara stared at him. "You started a war."

Barich shrugged. "I managed a risk."

CHAPTER TWENTY

The Children Were Never a Mystery

Jennifer's blood ran cold.

"The children," she said. "They weren't survivors."

Barich finally looked at her.

"No," he said. "They were *evidence*."

The room erupted.

"You let that ship be boarded!"

"You let people die!"

"You left children hiding in a reactor!"

Barich raised his voice for the first time. "I didn't *let* anything happen. I documented it."

Silence followed.

"The aliens boarded the Hammerhead," Barich continued. "Yes. They sabotaged it. Yes. But their mistake was not destroying it completely. The maintenance systems were meant to repair *any* damage, including conquest."

He gestured at the humming consoles.

"And now they've done exactly that."

Ryan looked sick. "You're going to wipe them out."

"No," Barich said. "I'm going to finish what they started."

CHAPTER TWENTY-ONE

Ground Truth

On the planet below, the alien stood exactly where they had last seen him.

Still angry.

Still gesturing at the soil.

He stabbed a clawed finger into the ground, shouting at his companion, his posture rigid with outrage. He wasn't defending territory.

He was defending his *home*.

Jennifer understood then.

"They weren't invaders," she said quietly. "They were trying to stop you."

Barich didn't deny it.

"They attacked a corporate asset," he said. "That makes them hostile."

Mara stepped forward. "You're about to deploy weapons from this ship, aren't you?"

Barich smiled again. "Terraforming equipment can be… repurposed."

The tanks had never been an invasion force.

They were **pre-positioned corporate security**.

CHAPTER TWENTY-TWO

Mutiny in Silence

The maintenance robots paused.

Just for a moment.

Ryan noticed.

So did Jennifer.

Barich frowned. “Why is my command queue delayed?”

Ryan smiled for the first time in minutes. “Because you forgot something.”

Barich turned slowly.

“You don’t actually know how this ship works,” Ryan said. “You know contracts. Not systems.”

Jennifer stepped beside him. “You woke the ship.”

Mara finished it. “But *we* taught it who to trust.”

The robots moved.

Not toward the crew.

Toward Barich.

“Impossible,” Barich snapped. “I have override.”

Ryan leaned close to the console and pressed one final control.

“No,” he said. “You had *permission*.”

The Hammerhead’s main display changed.

MAINTENANCE AUTHORITY — REVOKED
CREW SAFETY PROTOCOL — ACTIVE

Barich backed away.

For the first time, he looked afraid.

CHAPTER TWENTY-THREE

The Choice

They did not kill him.

They left him alive, locked in a sealed observation module, watching as the Hammerhead descended *without* firing a single weapon.

On the ground, the alien watched the sky warily.

Jennifer exited the ship first, hands open.

The alien began shouting immediately, angry, shrill, gesturing furiously at the soil again, then at the ship, then at *Barich's prison module*, visible through the hull window.

Ryan activated the translator.

"THIS ONE IS THE PROBLEM," the alien yelled. "WE TOLD YOU."

Jennifer nodded. "We know."

Behind her, the hibernating crew moved with confidence, now no longer lost, no longer innocent. They carried tools, not weapons. Engineers. Builders. Survivors.

The Space Pirate powered down, not as a weapon, but as a shelter.

Above them, the maintenance swarm repositioned not to attack, but to *protect*.

Barich watched it all from behind reinforced glass, finally understanding the truth:

The crew had stopped being expendable.

And the company had lost its ship.

CHAPTER TWENTY-FOUR

When Talking Fails

A human did not fire the first shot.

It came from the far edge of the valley, a thunderous crack that split the air and sent a plume of soil skyward. Alien armor surged out from concealed trenches and shattered structures, unfolding like a living machine that had been waiting for permission to breathe. The angry alien, still gesturing furiously at the ground, froze.

Then it screamed.

Not at the humans.

At its own people. The translator struggled, but the meaning was unmistakable.

"STOP, THEY ARE NOT"

The second impact silenced the rest.

Jennifer didn't wait for orders.

"DEFENSIVE POSITIONS!" she shouted.

The Space Pirate's landing lights flared as energy shields snapped online. The Space Pirate screamed overhead, engines howling, its shadow racing across the battlefield like a warning that came too late. Alien tanks rose from the earth itself, hatches snapping shut, weapons swiveling with terrifying precision. They weren't crude machines. They were elegant. Purpose-built.

This wasn't a skirmish.

It was a prepared response.

CHAPTER TWENTY-FIVE

Veterans Are Made Fast

The hibernation crew did not panic.

They should have, but they didn't. They moved with sharp efficiency, setting barricades, rerouting power, and deploying drones. Hands that had once fumbled with controls now worked smoothly, confidently, as if fear had burned itself out of them already.

Ryan coordinated fire lanes with a calm voice that surprised even him.

Mara dragged a wounded tech to cover without breaking stride.

Jennifer launched the Space Pirate again, dodging plasma fire so close it scorched the hull paint. She brought the ship around hard, fusion engines roaring, and opened fire on a column of advancing armor.

The impact lit the valley in blinding white.

Alien tanks shattered, flipping end over end.

And still they came.

CHAPTER TWENTY-SIX

The Ground Remembers Blood

The alien infantry advanced in disciplined waves, their weapons tearing through rock and steel alike. Humans returned fire, cut them down, but for every one that fell, two more rose from hidden tunnels and armored doors built into the planet itself.

The angry alien, now unbound, ran into the open.

Jennifer screamed at him to get back.

He ignored her, standing between both forces, arms wide, shouting until his voice broke. "THIS IS OUR SOIL, AND THEY ARE NOT THE ENEMY HE IS"

A shot took him in the chest. He collapsed into the dirt he had defended so fiercely.

For a moment, just a moment, everything stopped.

Then hell resumed.

CHAPTER TWENTY-SEVEN

Barich's Last Calculation

From his sealed observation module aboard the Hammerhead, Barich watched the battle unfold in cold silence.

Casualty estimates climbed.

Corporate projections collapsed.

"This was not the outcome," he muttered.

The Hammerhead did not respond.

Below, the maintenance swarm repositioned, not to protect corporate assets, but to shield evacuation routes. Automated systems diverted power away from weapons and into medical bays, life support, and atmosphere control.

Barich slammed his fist against the glass.

"You're wasting the investment!"

The ship ignored him.

It had learned something else mattered more.

CHAPTER TWENTY-EIGHT

The Turning Point

Ryan realized it first.

"They're not trying to win," he said. "They're trying to push us back."

Jennifer saw it too: alien units funneling humans away from population centers, herding rather than annihilating.

"They're defending," she said quietly.

Mara lowered her rifle slightly. "From us."

Jennifer made the call.

"All units pull fire. Defensive only. No pursuit."

Some hesitated.

Then they obeyed.

The Space Pirate broke off its attack run and climbed, engines screaming in protest.

Alien fire slackened.

Slowly, painfully, the battle unraveled into uneasy distance.

Smoke drifted across the valley.

Bodies lay on both sides. And in the silence that followed, everyone understood the same terrible truth.

This war had never needed to happen.

CHAPTER TWENTY-NINE

After the Noise

The Space Pirate stood quietly on the planet's surface.

Repaired.
Scarred.
Watching.

The humans buried their dead.

So did the aliens.

No treaties were signed. No victory claimed.

But weapons stayed lowered.

The hibernation crew gathered near the ship that night, exhausted and older than they had been that morning. They spoke softly, shared food, repaired armor, treated wounds, no longer passengers, no longer innocent.

They were crew now.

Survivors.

Jennifer stood beside Ryan, staring up at the stars.

"We came here to build something," Ryan said.

Jennifer nodded. "We almost destroyed it instead."

Behind them, the Hammerhead's lights dimmed to a soft glow, no longer an invasion vessel, no longer a corporate prize.

Just a ship.

Waiting.

CHAPTER THIRTY

The Sky Breaks First

The Hammerhead burned in orbit.

Not from damage, but from betrayal.

Alien boarding craft pierced its hull in silent waves, slipping past systems never meant to fight an enemy that knew the ship better than its builders. Maintenance corridors flooded with shapes that moved too fast, too precisely, disabling relays and severing control nodes with surgical intent.

On the planet below, Jennifer felt it before anyone said a word.

The sky changed.

A second sun appeared long, glowing, wrong, stretching across the upper atmosphere like a wound.

Ryan looked up slowly. "That's not a burn-up trail."

"No," Jennifer said. Her voice was hollow. "That's orbital decay."

The Hammerhead had been taken.

CHAPTER THIRTY-ONE

The Last Decision

Inside the ship, Barich screamed.

His prison module rattled as gravity fluctuated violently. He slammed his fists against the glass, shouting into an intercom that no one answered anymore.

"You can't do this! You'll destroy the asset!"

The aliens did not care.

They had learned the truth too late that the Hammerhead was not merely a ship, but a promise of endless arrival. Endless taking.

They had decided that the promise would end.

Alien hands forced the final command.

Thrusters fired not to stabilize orbit, but to *break it.*

The Hammerhead turned, nose angling toward the planet it had nearly claimed.

And began to fall.

CHAPTER THIRTY-TWO

Evacuation Is a Lie

Alarms screamed across every channel.

The crew ran.

The Space Pirate lifted off under full power, overloaded with survivors, engines screaming in protest as debris began to rain from the sky. Flaming fragments tore through clouds, lighting the world in streaks of white fire.

Jennifer strapped herself into the pilot's seat, hands steady despite the shaking hull.

"How much time?" Ryan asked.

Jennifer didn't look back. "Not enough." Behind them, the Hammerhead entered the atmosphere. Its massive structure glowed molten gold, greenhouses tearing free and scattering like falling stars. One cylinder ruptured completely, oceans flashing to steam in an instant.

The ship roared.

Not like a machine.

Like something dying.

CHAPTER THIRTY-THREE

Impact

The Hammerhead struck beyond the horizon.

The world shook.

A shockwave rolled across the land, flattening forests, collapsing alien structures, and ripping soil from the ground down to bedrock. The sky turned white, then black.

Jennifer fought the controls as the Space Pirate was thrown violently sideways, slamming into the ground hard enough to snap restraints and knock the breath from her chest.

Silence followed.

Long.
Absolute.

When the dust cleared, a new mountain rose where the Hammerhead had fallen, still glowing, still burning, still reshaping the planet forever.

The colonization ship had become a scar.

CHAPTER THIRTY-FOUR

After the End

They stood together at the edge of the devastation.

Humans.
Aliens.

No weapons raised.

No shouting.

The angry alien, the one who had screamed and gestured and warned, knelt and pressed its hands into the ground. It did not yell now.

It mourned.

Ryan broke the silence. “No one won.”

The alien looked at him, eyes dark and exhausted. “NO,” it said quietly. “BUT IT IS OVER.”

Jennifer watched smoke rise from the impact zone, her reflection trembling in her helmet visor.

The Hammerhead was gone.

The company’s dream was gone.

And with it, the lie that had brought them all here.

CHAPTER THIRTY-FIVE

What Remains

The survivors rebuilt slowly.

Together.

The hibernation crew no longer innocent, no longer afraid, became leaders, teachers, planners. Humans learned to use the land instead of reshaping it. The aliens learned to fear the strangers rather than fear them. The Hammerhead was permanently grounded, engines stripped for parts, and the hull converted into a shelter.

Above them, the sky was empty.

No ships waited there now.

No promises fell from orbit.

Only the future they would have to build with their own hands.

And far away, beneath layers of cooling stone, the Hammerhead slept its last act not conquest, but warning.

The End

Author qualifications

2015 Master of Laws [LLM]

Australian National University, Acton, ACT

2015 Graduate Diploma of Legal Practice [GDLP]

Australian National University, Acton, ACT

2013 Juris Doctor [JD]

Murdoch University, Perth, WA

2005 Master of Business Administration, Entrepreneurship & Finance (Adv) [MBA (Adv)]

UWA, Graduate School of Management, Perth, WA

1998 Bachelor of Electrical & Electronic Engineering, Control Systems (Hons) [BE (Hons)]

UWA, Centre for Intelligent Information Processing Systems (CIIPS), Perth, WA